BODYGUARD

BAD BOYS IN BIG TROUBLE 3

FIONA ROARKE

BODYGUARD
Bad Boys in Big Trouble 3

Copyright © 2016 Fiona Roarke

This book is a work of fiction. The characters, organizations, events, and places portrayed in this book are products of the author's imagination and are either fictitious or are used fictitiously. Any similarity to a real person, living or dead is purely coincidental and not intended by the author.

Nickel Road Publishing
ISBN: 978-1-944312-05-3

Published in the United States of America

DEDICATION

For my husband who keeps me sane when life tries to take me around the bend and off the rails.

The baseball stadium is torture for Chloe Wakefield, from the noisy stands to the slimy man her colleague set her up with.

Too bad she isn't with the sexy stud seated on her other side. He shares his popcorn. Shields her from the crowd. And, when the kiss cam swings their way, gives her a lip-lock that knocks her socks into the next county.

Goodbye, vile blind date. Hello, gorgeous stranger.

Staying under the radar is pretty much a job requisite for bodyguard Deke Langston, but he can't resist tasting Chloe's sweet lips. Nor her sweet invitation into her bed, where the sensuous little virgin proceeds to blow his mind.

But someone doesn't like how close they are getting. The thought that scares Deke the most is that another woman in his care might be hurt because of his past.

All of Deke's skills are put to the test as he and Chloe race to solve the puzzle of who is plotting against them.

Chloe's in danger and Deke has never had a more precious body to guard.

Bodyguard, Bad Boys in Big Trouble 3
Nothing's sexier than a good man gone bad boy.

CHAPTER 1

"So…what do you want for breakfast?"

"What?" Chloe Wakefield hadn't been paying attention to her loathsome date in the chaos of her surroundings. She was sure her co-worker meant well, but the blind date she'd set Chloe up with tonight was truly the definition of vile.

From Ned honking his car horn outside her house until she opened her front door to see who was making the racket, to his trying to impress her with "expensive seats" at a loud, crowd-filled baseball game, Chloe planned to give Justine an earful Monday morning at work about Ned the Neanderthal.

"Breakfast," he said, narrowing his eyes. "It's the most important meal of the day, according to some."

"Why?" she asked as someone from the row behind them bumped a boney knee into her shoulder, sending a spasm of discomfort down her spine. She really didn't like crowds. Justine supposedly told this guy Chloe didn't like being around lots of people. So spending their time together in a stadium full of loud baseball fans was like a nightmare on steroids she couldn't wake up from.

Note to self: No more blind date opportunities from Justine. Ever.

"To make sure I have it on hand," Ned said slyly.

Chloe, preoccupied with the literally thousands of loud people around her, asked the same two questions again, only together this time. "What? Why?"

Ned turned in his seat to face her. "Are you dense? So I can make us breakfast in the morning! Sheesh. What is wrong with you?" He put his arm around the back of her seat, moving into her already limited personal space and pressing close. That did not help her claustrophobic issues at all. Not to mention the cologne he must have bathed in—likely masking the scent of brimstone—made her want to breathe through her mouth.

She turned to face him, pressing backward into the edge of the molded seat next to hers to escape his familiarity.

"I don't understand. Why would you make breakfast for me?" She moved so far away from her date that she pushed one shoulder blade solidly into the arm of the stranger seated to her left. He didn't seem to mind or at least he didn't say anything as she crowded him. Plus, he smelled good. Something she noted before putting her focus back on Ned. He didn't smell nearly as nice and seemed peeved at her for some reason.

"Let me spell it out for you, sweet cheeks. Justine implied you were a sure thing. So after the game I'd planned to take you to my place for a quick roll in the hay. If you want to spend the night and screw more than just once, even better, and I thought I'd be nice enough to provide a morning meal afterward if you stayed over. Is *that* clear enough for you?"

Chloe had pushed so far back into the stranger's shoulder, she was practically sharing his seat with him. She was grateful he wasn't scolding her or shoving her back into her own seat. "Yes. Crystal. So let me be equally clear. I am *not* having sex with you tonight or any other night."

Ned's brows furrowed, but not in confusion. He understood. "Is that so?" he asked in a low, tight voice.

"Yes. So no breakfast needed, right?"

He nodded, but his angry expression intensified. "I only sprang for these pricy seats because you were supposed to put out."

Sucks to be you, she thought, but didn't feel the need to apologize. Chloe stared straight into his beady little eyes and shrugged without a single iota of remorse. He couldn't get physical with all the people around, making her glad for the crowd for the first time this evening.

Ned the Neanderthal grunted, retreated and turned his back on her. Two seconds later he was flirting with the two girls seated to his right, ignoring Chloe as if she didn't exist.

Thankfully, now she was all alone in a sea of humanity. That presented a new challenge, though. It had been difficult enough getting to the "pricy" seats in the first place, inching their way past a dozen people who were already seated.

Chloe didn't relish trying to extract herself anytime soon. Pushing past nimrod, his two giggling new girlfriends and several more people was a task she simply couldn't face just yet.

The fact that the hair on the back of her neck had been standing at attention all night like something was out of place should have been an early warning signal to forgo this blind date. Only the promise she'd made to Justine—or rather blood oath she'd practically been forced to swear—to go on a date for once and have some fun had brought her here tonight.

The uneasy feeling lurking in the back of her mind for no obvious reason wouldn't dissipate. It was probably the noisy, exuberant crowd that was making her nervous. She inhaled deeply and let her breath out slowly. She needed to calm her racing heart.

Not to mention her idiot date had driven her here. She couldn't leave until he did. So Chloe got used to the idea of waiting until the stadium emptied after the game before moving again.

"Want some popcorn?" a sultry, sexy voice from over her shoulder asked. That made her realize she was still pressed against the nice-smelling stranger beside her.

With her date leaning away from her like she'd been suddenly struck with leprosy, Chloe retreated to the center of her own seat and swiveled around to get a better look at Mr. Smell Good.

At first glance she thought, *Oh my, he's gorgeous*.

Then he smiled, putting him in a whole new league of attractive.

Chloe had stared first at his luscious brown eyes, until she saw his sexy, kissable mouth. *Oh my*. Her gaze drifted down a delectable muscular body that included flat abs encased in a snug blue T-shirt and made a return to his face. The popcorn bag he held was open in her direction. She shook off her instant lust and grabbed a handful of salty snack. "Thank you."

"My pleasure." *Oh my*. That sexy voice would live in her dreams.

"I'm Chloe," she managed to say before chickening out.

"Deke." He held out his hand. She grasped it and shook his firm, callused fingers, wanting to hold hands for the rest of the game. He looked deeply into her eyes as if acknowledging there might be something already very special between them. Her gaze in return was as intense as she dared given that he was a stranger. He'd treated her better in ten seconds than her date had all night.

Her special, private list of attributes for a member of the male species worthy enough to grace her bed came to mind. This sexy stranger was definitely a contender. Chloe leaned closer, unable to stop staring, still grasping his hand in hers. He didn't look away either. Nor did he release her fingers.

The loud crack echoing across the ballpark disrupted their special moment as the entire stadium came to their feet to watch the first home run of the game sail into the left-field bleachers on the other side of the park.

Neither of them moved, remaining cocooned by the standing, cheering people in their section. That was almost too much for Chloe. A flash of panic struck. She glanced around as she was trapped in her seat, unable to see anything or move anywhere, but for the first time in a long while she didn't care. Her gaze found Deke's again. Their palms were still attached. He somehow soothed her with a mere look.

Then the man to Deke's left bent down and asked, "Did you see that? First hit, right out of the park. Amazing."

Deke glanced over his shoulder, breaking the intense gaze they'd shared briefly to nod once in his friend's direction. Chloe knew he hadn't seen anything because he'd been watching her. And she'd been watching him. And best of all they'd been grasping each other's hands, while tucked among the others in a quiet little moment. Her, like it was a lifeline for survival. Him, like maybe he wanted to caress her soul. She wanted to let him.

After everyone sat back down, Chloe leaned close to whisper into his ear, "I'm sorry you missed it."

"I'm not." He grinned. "I *am* sorry your boyfriend is such a dick though."

Chloe laughed. "He's not my boyfriend. He's a horrible blind date I was set up with by someone I *thought* I could trust. I won't make that mistake again."

That made *him* laugh. Deke had a great laugh.

"Are you even a baseball fan?" Deke asked. The scent of his yummy cologne washed over her each time he moved near to converse.

She shrugged. "Baseball is okay. I'm more of a football fan. But either way I prefer cheering from my living room sofa." She glanced around her immediate space. "It's quieter."

"Good answer." He offered her the popcorn bag again.

She took another handful. "Is it?"

He nodded. "I feel the exact same way."

"Why are you here, then?"

He frowned at first and then caught himself. Nodding his head in the direction of the guy he was seated next to, Deke said, "I'm here doing a favor for a friend."

Another loud crack came and this time they stood with the crowd. She gasped and held onto his arm as her anxiety of being crushed by the people surrounding her rose up, ready to choke her with unreasonable fear.

Deke pulled his arm from her tight hold. Drat. But then he quickly circled it around her shoulders, pulling her into his muscular frame as if to comfort her. She really needed it.

"You're trembling," he said in a surprised tone. "Are you okay?"

She nodded just a little. "I'm not a huge fan of crowds, but you make it bearable. So thanks." Chloe looked deeply into his sultry bedroom-brown eyes and he moved closer, his hand already tangled in her hair, squeezing her shoulder. Was he about to kiss her? Yes!

His friend crashed an elbow into Deke's arm. "Did you see that hit? Right out of the park. This is an excellent game!"

Deke glanced at the other man and smiled, but also quickly removed his arm from around Chloe as if he might get caught in an intimate, compromising position. Getting Deke into any kind of compromising position held a certain appeal.

They and the rest of the stadium sat as the game

continued on the field below. Deke didn't move away from her, but he chatted with his friend for a few minutes. He was, after all, here with someone else.

Chiding herself for lusting after a virtual stranger, Chloe took a deep breath and chilled her attitude. Deke wasn't her date. He wasn't supposed to be entertaining her.

After a few minutes, he offered her more popcorn. He leaned his head close to hers every few minutes to whisper in her ear and comment on various things not necessarily to do with baseball. It was intimate and she liked it very much.

He was charming and funny and a much better date than the slime she'd come here with. Each time she chanced a glance at his full sculpted mouth, she could hardly stop staring. By the time the fourth inning rolled around, Chloe was more than half in love with her beautiful stranger. She'd checked several attributes off on her special private list, as well.

She glanced at Ned periodically. He continued to ignore her, embroiled with those two giggling girls and acted as if he hadn't brought her here tonight. Good. She decided to pretend she wasn't with him either, shifting in her seat so she was closer to Deke.

Deke turned toward her, leaning in again like each time they talked it had to be clandestine. "Want some water?" He gestured subtly toward the vendor at the end of their row selling cold bottles.

"Yes. Please." He signaled for two and paid for them, shaking his head at her offer to pay him back. "My treat," he said, and handed her an icy plastic bottle along with a sexy grin.

She saw movement from the corner of her eye. It was the large screen in the stadium. The image swept over the audience at a fast clip as if searching for someone, then suddenly came to a stop on a couple holding bottles of water and smiling at each other as if they shared a secret.

"Oh my! That's us," she whispered, slightly alarmed. Below the Jumbotron frame were the words, *Kiss Cam*.

Deke looked at the big screen and turned back to her with a grin. "Should we?" he asked, staring at her like she was the only person in the whole stadium.

Chloe didn't answer. Instead, she moved her face forward until their lips met. *Oh my.* Firm but yielding, his lips were delectable. A rush of pleasure skated down her spine as the kiss continued. Deke slanted his mouth sideways to deepen this first connection. Boy howdy, could he kiss.

She pressed her mouth even harder to his luscious lips, like she'd wanted to do since he offered her popcorn. His hand came up and cupped the side of her head, pressing his mouth firmly into the kiss as if she'd break away before he was ready to let her go. He had nothing to worry about. She might not ever let go or stop kissing him.

The world she was barely paying attention to fell away as this perfect first kiss continued. His fingers drifted from her face and into her hair, gripping her tresses lightly as if to keep her in place. She liked it. He tasted as good as he smelled, a little salty and maybe a little dangerous. Or perhaps her fanciful mind imagined things.

Deke's friend laughed and said, "Good for you, Deke. FYI, the camera has moved on to another couple." Then he laughed again.

At the same time, Ned said, "Are you effing kidding me?" He pushed her shoulder hard with his sharp forefinger, breaking the amazing lip lock.

Deke grabbed Ned's finger and wrapped his fist around it, throwing the other man's whole hand away. "Don't touch her."

"What the hell? She's *my* date!"

"As if," Chloe said. "You've ignored me this whole game. How is this remotely still a date? Go back to your giggly new girlfriends."

"Fine. I will. And since you're not my date anymore, you can find your own way home." An oily little smile of superiority shaped his thin lips. She knew it was because he had told her not to bring a purse, that she wouldn't need it for where they were going. He thought he was stranding her.

Chloe stilled. In a small leather bifold wallet she usually carried while exercising, currently resting in the back pocket of her jeans hugged up against her phone, she'd shoved her driver's license alongside the ten-dollar bill and spare key already tucked inside.

Ten dollars probably wasn't enough to get a cab out of the ball park, let alone all the way to her house. She cursed herself silently for trusting the man Justine had set her up with. Likely she'd be walking a fair distance tonight unless she could catch a ride. Or she'd call Justine and demand an extraction from this horrendous blind date she'd set in motion.

Chloe folded her arms, turned and stared out at the field. It was the end of the inning. One team raced away and into their dugout while the opposing team ran onto the field to their appointed places, mitts in hand.

Deke put a hand on her arm. She looked into his troubled expression. "If I could take you home myself, I would." He glanced over his shoulder. "However, I didn't drive here alone tonight or in my vehicle. We carpooled."

Her luscious dream man was about to abandon her, too. It was too much. She nodded and shot him a timid smile of understanding. It wasn't his responsibility to ensure she made it home safe and sound. But then her eyes welled up. "Don't worry. I'll figure it out," she managed without sobbing aloud, but it wasn't easy.

"Hey, no. It's not like that. I'll make sure you get home. I promise. Might have to be a taxi though, okay?"

"You don't have to worry. Seriously, it's not your place."

"Sure it is."

"Why?"

"Because I kissed you back. And I liked it." He had seemed just as deeply involved in that kiss as she had been while thousands watched. Maybe they did have more than just a casual connection. She felt her lips wobble.

Yes. He'd definitely kissed her back.

She blinked and spilled teardrops on both cheeks, half in joy, half in relief. Deke wiped one away with his thumb and then the other. "The thing is, technically, I'm working tonight."

"You are?" She sniffed, wiped her eyes, and smiled. "What…um…what do you do?"

Those luscious eyes bored a hole into her soul. "Bodyguard."

Ah, the danger I tasted in your kiss.

CHAPTER 2

Chloe's smile punched Deke right in the gut. Her green eyes and dark hair had mesmerized him since she'd grabbed that first handful of popcorn. His mind went on vacation whenever he looked her way. It was partly her long wavy hair and girl next door appeal. He was a sucker for brunettes, and girl next door types. Her vulnerability was also something he could never ignore, especially in the face of her date's bad behavior.

Deke wasn't really supposed to announce his occupation to just anyone, and especially not when he was working, but his brain was unable to function correctly when the tantalizing scent of her distracted him, like it had been all night.

The kiss, while ranked easily one of the top three in his life, had been off the charts in regrettable career behavior. He shouldn't have done it for a number of reasons. Those details had all been playing over and over in his head after he'd foolishly asked her, "Should we?" like he was free to kiss beautiful green-eyed brunettes at baseball games and forget he was currently on the job.

The guy he was sitting next to was a good friend, but

more an employer tonight. Deke was only an extra body to go along with the two primary bodyguards detailed to Garrick this evening. Still, he was here because they needed a third qualified bodyguard to satisfy an insurance policy.

They weren't expecting any specific trouble. It was more of a show to keep the crowd at a distance as they entered and exited the premises rather than *dive in front of a bullet* sort of protection.

Either way, if Deke had been in charge, he wouldn't have let his friend come to the game at all unless they were in box seats behind safety glass. But that hadn't been his call.

Plus, Garrick liked to sit in the stands "like a regular Joe," as he put it. And serendipity had put Deke directly next to Chloe. He certainly wouldn't thumb his nose at fate.

Chloe stared, wide eyed. "Bodyguard?"

"Yeah. Why? Is that a deal breaker?"

She sucked in a deep breath. "No. It's…uh…well…it's good." She seemed to stumble to come up with the word.

"*Good*, huh? What were you going to say?"

She grinned. "Sexy as hell."

"Not the reality of it, but—"

Garrick's nudge interrupted his explanation, and Deke turned to him. His friend leaned in and spoke in a low tone. "Take her home, Deke. I don't really need a third man after we leave the game anyway. She can ride back with us to where your car is parked."

"Are you certain? I don't want to leave you low manned."

"You're not. You were here more as my guest than my protection detail anyway. Be a hero. Take her home. It's obvious you two have quite a spark between you. I only ask to be best man at the wedding."

"Whoa. That's quite a leap, Garrick."

He laughed. "I saw that lip lock, my friend, on the big screen no less. You two practically set the stadium on fire with that kiss cam shot." He winked and nodded as if he approved.

Deke rolled his eyes. Garrick whole-heartedly believed in love at first sight. He and his wife had been married for over thirty years after only knowing each other for a few weeks. Deke knew, because Garrick and his wife were very good friends with his parents.

He turned to Chloe and smiled. "Looks like I'm off the hook."

"You're not fired, are you?"

"No. Nothing like that. I was doing a favor. Now he's doing me one."

They settled back in their seats to watch the rest of the game, but Deke experienced the nagging feeling that he was either missing something important or someone was watching them. He cast a professional glance around their immediate surroundings, seeing an ocean of people but no obvious threat.

The stadium crowd and broadcast viewing audience at home had gotten quite an eyeful of them kissing. Maybe that was where his anxiety rested. He didn't typically care to be the center of attention. In his profession, being the focus of any public situation could be deadly. He much preferred being invisible to those around him in all scenarios.

Oftentimes it was difficult to turn off bodyguard mode. He truly needed to have it on and fully functional right now. His gut was only registering a midrange panic, riding the fence like an indecisive patron unwilling to jump into a growing barroom brawl.

The phone in his pocket buzzed. It was a text from his brother, Zak.

I saw that kiss on the big screen, bro.
Who's the chick?
Thought you were working tonight.
Isn't that why *I'm* not there right now?

Deke pushed out a long sigh. His brother was a big fan of the Arizona home team playing tonight. He was likely kicked back watching the game on his sofa because coming here with Garrick had caused a mock fight between them.

Zak wasn't a bodyguard, but he'd wanted to go in Deke's place. Deke had turned him down. It wasn't that Zak couldn't handle the job. In fact, until recently his brother had worked undercover. That was how he'd met his new wife—by posing as a biker infiltrating a gang. He'd been part of a clandestine group called The Organization, a private security firm of sorts. There was a time when he and Zak rarely communicated, especially after they'd moved away from home and on to their busy lives. Nowadays, he and Zak talked at least once a week.

So it wasn't such a shock to hear from him anymore, since he also didn't work undercover as often.

Deke sent him a brief text in reply.

Long story. We'll talk later.

Zak texted back.

Yes. We will. I require explanations.
Or else the recorded kiss video goes to the 'rents.

If Zak had seen him kiss Chloe, and was threatening to send the provocative footage to their parents, Deke wondered how many others had seen him. *Millions?* Great.

Pushing out a long sigh, Deke watched the rest of the

game with the added bonus of unease tickling the back of his mind after his blatant public display. He shouldn't have drawn attention to himself while sitting next to Garrick. Now his innate senses would roil in speculation of who might have seen them and have enough balls to do something about it.

Sometimes gut feelings were a big pain in the ass.

In the middle of the eighth inning, Garrick got a call and had to leave the game. The home team he rooted for was several runs ahead, but Deke knew his friend hated to leave before the very end.

The only good news was the traffic exiting the parking lot would be less harrowing.

Deke turned to Chloe. "Hey. Unfortunately, we have to leave early. Still want a ride home?" His gaze went to her date, who was drooling like a letch over the two girls seated next to him.

Chloe didn't bother taking a peek over her shoulder. "Absolutely."

"I hate for you to miss the rest of the game."

"Trust me. I didn't want to come here in the first place. While I'm glad I did, because I met you, I can't wait to get out of here."

They carefully moved past the other spectators, but Deke let Chloe go ahead of him, wanting to protect her back from her odious blind date. The man had turned to stare daggers at her until Deke blocked his view and exited the row. Good riddance.

The short walk to the exit was spent in silence, although Garrick was on the phone with someone arranging to meet at his office. Perfect, since that was where Deke's car was parked. He'd get them a lift in the limo and take Chloe home from there.

One of the primary guards had called ahead to Garrick's driver and the opulent ride was waiting curbside. The driver came around and opened the rear door. Garrick gestured for Chloe to get in first, but she simply stared at the open door and remained on the curb.

Deke walked two steps toward her. "My friend has to go back to his office a few miles from here, which is also where my car is parked. I thought we'd catch a ride with them and then I'll take you home myself."

She stared at Deke with a wide-eyed, fearful look. "I thought you were getting me a taxi." Shaking her head, she added, "I'm sorry, but I don't want to get in a vehicle with strangers."

Chloe didn't have any negative instincts about Deke or his friend, whom she recognized as an exemplary elected leader in their community, but getting into a vehicle, even a limo, with people she didn't know very well was foolish from her point of view.

Perhaps her job as a real estate agent had jaded her to the idea of even meeting strangers without another agent along or at least several of her colleagues apprised of her whereabouts. An armed escort would be nice to bring along at each showing too, but she couldn't afford it.

"Listen, I appreciate what you did in the stands for me, but the truth is I don't know you. In fact, I don't even know your last name."

He smiled a beautiful and understanding sexy half-smile that made her knees weaken. "It's Langston. Deke Langston."

His friend said, "You know who I am, though, right? Garrick Austin Mason. I can vouch for Deke, if that would help."

Chloe considered his offer. She did know who he was publicly, but not privately. "I know of you," she said cautiously, glancing over one shoulder at the taxi stand with one lonely cab driver in line. "And I've seen you in the media. However, we've also never met before."

"Tell me what to do to put your mind at ease and I'll do it," Deke said.

She knew exactly what to do. It was what she did with every potential real estate client. She was aware of the other two men, bodyguards like Deke, she assumed, keeping a watchful eye on their surroundings while they all stood beside the waiting limo. "Hang on. Let me check something."

Pulling her phone out of her back pocket, Chloe put his name in a well-known search engine, seeking any kind of information that he was a serial killer or wanted for any heinous crimes. His identity popped up with lots of information about his profession as a bodyguard along with several images of his handsome face.

"Wow. You're famous. You're the one who saved that school bus full of kids from a maniac and also that singer with the twin stalkers."

"Yes. Well, that was a couple of years ago."

Chloe put her phone back in her pocket. "Okay. Let's go. I just didn't want to be considered too stupid to live, climbing into a car with veritable strangers."

"Understandable." He held out his hand and she took it, grateful to be in good hands, protection-wise anyway.

The two other guards got in right after Garrick was seated in back. Deke gestured for Chloe to get in ahead of him. Instead of climbing in behind her, he stood like a sentry by the door as if surveying the surrounding area for bad guys.

Likely an instinctual thing for him to do.

Garrick leaned forward in his seat and asked Deke, "Problem?"

"No, I'm just checking the area, making sure no one is checking us out." He ducked down to look into the limo. "I don't want to be too stupid to live either."

Deke finally climbed in and sat next to her along the driver's side of the limo, grabbing her hand and sandwiching it between both of his for the journey.

Garrick's phone rang again. He answered and got into a long conversation. The two bodyguards spoke quietly at the front of the limo.

Chloe turned to Deke and said, "Thank you."

"For?"

"Understanding my caution."

"I applaud it. More people should be like you."

"Also, thanks for taking me home." He squeezed her fingers gently in response, nodding lightly and smiling like he wanted to kiss her again. She stared back, giving him every opportunity to do so. It wasn't like they hadn't already kissed in front of tens of thousands of baseball fans tonight. He seemed content just to stare deeply into her eyes.

The intensity of his look smoldered with dark promises of passion, making her insides tingle and long for further attention. After several moments he said, "I'm glad we met tonight."

"Me, too. It makes going out with Ned a smart move on my part."

Deke laughed. "I almost didn't accept Garrick's invitation. That would have been a huge mistake."

"I guess it was fate." Chloe contemplated getting to know Deke better. She couldn't wait. She broke the stare to lean against him, the side of her face pressed against his shoulder. He squeezed her fingers tighter as if he approved.

Once he took her home, perhaps she'd invite him in.

The limo took a quick turn and then another, driving down a slope and slowing to a stop.

The two guards exited first, and then Garrick and finally Chloe and Deke climbed out of the luxury vehicle and into an underground parking structure.

"Thanks, Deke. Maybe next time we can actually stay for the whole game."

Deke laughed. "I won't hold my breath on that one. I'm surprised we lasted as long as we did tonight."

"You and me both." Garrick held out his hand to Chloe. "Nice to meet you, young lady. Deke's a good guy. Take it from me. You won't find better."

"Thanks, and also for the ride in a limo. It was my first time."

The two other guards and Garrick walked to an elevator. Deke took her hand and led her in the opposite direction to a row of vehicles nearby.

From his pocket he retrieved a fob, clicked a button and the lights flashed on a sexy sports car parked in the middle of the row.

Chloe said, "And here I figured you for the full-sized, fully-loaded SUV two spaces further down."

He laughed. "Guess what—my other car *is* a full-sized, fully-loaded SUV. Maybe you should think about a career as a spy. You're good at reading people."

"I do have a job where it helps to read people."

"You know," he said reaching for the passenger door handle, "it occurs to me that I don't know your last name or your profession either. You do look familiar to me for some reason. Anything I need to know?"

He released the door handle without opening it, a guarded smile playing over his luscious lips. "In the spirit of getting into a car with someone I don't know very well either, who are you? What do you do?"

"I'm Chloe Wakefield." She stuck her hand out. "I'm a real estate agent with Premier Housing. Hopefully that's not a deal breaker for you."

He took her hand, brushing a thumb gently along her forefinger to the first knuckle. Pleasure spiraled through her at his light touch.

Deke snapped his fingers. "I've seen your picture on

the house for sale at the end of my street."

She inhaled deeply, grateful that he hadn't sneered at her profession or even hinted at a negative remark. "I don't know where you live, but I've just narrowed it to seven places where I have my personal real estate agent sign hanging up."

"Madrid Avenue," he squeezed her fingers and leaned down to open the passenger door again.

"Nice neighborhood," she remarked, moving toward the open door. "If you ever want to sell, I'm your girl."

"I'll keep that in mind." He released her fingers. "Also, your profession is not a deal breaker." He made a face, as if asking, *Why would your perfectly acceptable profession be a deal breaker*, earning her gratitude and another checkmark on her private list.

Only the car door stood between them. "I'm glad," she whispered, waiting for what might happen next. *Kiss me.* As if reading her thoughts, he leaned in and kissed her upturned mouth.

Exactly like the kiss in the baseball stadium, this one lit her up like a flamethrower dropped on a pool of gasoline, He broke away sooner than she wanted, and said, "I should get you home like I promised. Where do you live?"

Still floating on a cloud of longing from his most recent amazing lip lock, she recited her address. "I know the area. You'll have to direct me when we get close." She nodded and slid inside his low-slung sports car. The molded leather seat hugged her body. Even his sports car seemed to embrace her lovingly. He closed her door, moving around the back of the vehicle to the driver's side. Deke's car smelled delicious, just like he did.

He got behind the wheel and they headed for her home. He drove beyond the edge of the speed limits all the way there, but he was a focused driver rather than distracted. Two minutes into the ride, she trusted him implicitly.

Chloe directed him to pull into the semi-circular driveway in front of her house.

"Would you like to come in for a cup of coffee or a night cap or something?" *Whatever I have that you want is yours for the asking.*

"A cup of coffee sounds great."

She reached for the door handle as she stared at him. He said, "Hang on for a minute, okay?" He exited the car and walked slowly around the front of his vehicle, eyes searching the surrounding area as if expecting trouble.

Her only trouble was a recent blind date idiot who was unlikely to ever darken her doorstep again. She was totally fine with that, making a mental note to discuss Justine's taste in men with her at the office next week.

Deke opened her door for her like a gentleman and reached for her hand to help her climb out of his car. She felt like a princess.

Chloe dug the bifold wallet out of her back pocket and removed the spare key, unlocked the door and ushered Deke inside her tidy, modest, two-story tract house. It wasn't huge like the houses in his neighborhood, but she loved it, having purchased it for an amazing price after only six months as a real estate agent. The acquisition made her feel not only successful, but like a grown up.

She secured the deadbolt, turned to his grinning face and said, "I'll make us a pot of coffee."

He nodded. "Mind if I use your bathroom?"

She directed him to the main one upstairs, as it was more spacious than the half-bath downstairs or even her master bathroom.

Four years in a growing real estate market had been very prosperous for Chloe and she was proud of her accomplishment. But her success hadn't come without sacrifices, namely dating. The fiasco with Ned reminded

Chloe exactly why it had been so long since she'd gone out with anyone.

Previous dates in her admittedly limited relationship history had yielded two types of men. Guys on the make and ready to jump in bed before they'd barely exchanged names or disinterested wretches unable to stay off their phones long enough to converse like human beings. Nothing in between.

Justine had tried to set her up on a number of blind dates in the last couple of years, but Chloe was busy tending to her career and didn't want to take the time to nurture a relationship that usually turned out poorly. Like tonight with Ned. Besides, why bother dating until she was ready to settle down?

After endless conversations with Justine about getting too old to attract a man, dying alone as an old maid, or forgetting how good sex could be, Chloe had accidently let it slip that she hadn't ever had sex and therefore wasn't missing anything.

It wasn't that she was particularly saving herself for marriage, although that's exactly what she confided to her parents through private chats with her mother. Unfortunately, her mom became another source of endless blind date proposals during holiday visits, romantic opportunities she'd mostly turned down, but had also endured for years.

Because Chloe saw Justine every day, her attempts were more difficult to refuse. Chloe had finally been worn down enough to accept a date with a guy Justine considered a successful, attractive entrepreneur anyone would be lucky to snag. After less than an hour in his company, Chloe disagreed. But fate smiled on her, giving her a reprieve from certain disaster in the form of the sexy bodyguard she'd lured home.

Tonight might be the start of something amazing.

CHAPTER 3

The coffee was brewing when Deke entered her kitchen. "I like your house," he said. "Very secure."

She laughed, turning her attention from the coffeemaker to her gorgeous guest. "Well, it was also a great price for this neighborhood and my budget at the time."

"You would know about that. I can only tell you the strength and weakness of the security." He walked over to the back door leading to the patio and tested that it was locked. "Deadbolt. Good. Lock actually in place. Excellent. Locked up tight during an evening out. Stupendous. I'm giving you high marks all around."

"Why spend the money on a deadbolt if you don't use it?"

"You'd be amazed what people do, don't do, and then wonder why they get robbed."

She shrugged. "I'm a girl and I live alone. Plus, I'm in real estate. I like the homes I sell to be secure, so I practice what I preach."

"Good for you. I'm impressed."

The coffee finished brewing. She poured a cup, put it in front of him near the cream and sugar and then fixed one for herself. He picked it up without adding anything and drank it black. Before she finished doctoring hers, he moved close to tower over her. He had to be eight inches taller than her five-foot-six height, but she liked looking up at him.

"Thanks for the coffee. It's good and strong, just the way I like it."

She could get lost in his gaze. Shaking off her lust, Chloe tore her attention from him and went back to making her coffee. She loaded lots of cream and sugar into her cup.

"Are you making a cake in there or something?" he teased, sipping his own coffee.

Chloe grinned. *Sense of humor. Check.* One more attribute fulfilled on her list. "I just like my coffee strong, creamy and sweet. Problem with that?"

"Nope." He smiled like he was amused or perhaps she charmed him. That's what she wanted to do. Charm him into further kisses. Maybe she could charm him into more than just lip locks on her living room sofa. Maybe she'd invite him upstairs for a tour of her bedroom sheets.

She led him into the next room and gestured to the sofa. When he sat she settled down close to him, put her cup on the table and turned sideways to face him. No doubt about it. Deke was a worthy contender for her special private list.

He was a gentleman, opening doors for her and the like.

He protected her from Ned and rescued her from walking home alone.

He liked her coffee. She was lumping that in with having him like her cooking.

He was employed in a job he was obviously very good at, being famous online and all.

His kisses knocked her socks into the next county.

He was taller than her. His physical attractiveness was a side attribute to consider, but she figured it was too shallow to add to her top ten.

He also didn't denigrate her career. That had happened a lot on previous dates, setups or not. Several of the men she'd gone out with before snickered when she told them her occupation, deciding that being a Realtor meant that she wasn't smart enough for a "real" job. Apparently, all the Realtors her previous idiot dates knew were middle aged women looking for something to occupy their time once their kids were out of the house.

Deke was the top contender on her private list.

A childhood with nice memories, a good relationship with his parents, and getting along with his siblings were all that remained standing between them and ending up in her bedroom tonight.

With a score of seven out of ten so far, she was likely going to lure him upstairs anyway. The last several guys she'd gone out with didn't score higher than three after more than one date.

She wanted so much for Deke to be the one—the man who fit her specially crafted list of worthy attributes for *finally* giving up her virginity.

"Tell me about your family," she said. "Do your parents live nearby? Any siblings?"

"My parents live in New Mexico. And I have four brothers. We're pretty tight, although we don't see each other as often as we'd like."

"Wow. Five boys? How is your mother doing after living with all that testosterone?"

"She's likely tired," he said with a laugh. "She's also probably glad we're all out of her hair, but she'd never say that. In fact, she cried when every single one of us moved out."

"That's sweet. It's my idea of exactly what moms are supposed to do."

"I agree. So what about you? Do your parents live in the area? Any siblings?"

"My parents used to live in Tennessee—that's where I grew up—but they retired to Florida a couple of years ago. I have two brothers. One is older and married with three kids, and the other one younger and in college with a pretty serious girlfriend."

"Are your brothers protective of you?"

Chloe shrugged. "When I was in high school, my older brother was known to snarl at the occasional date picking me up, but not lately."

"So, for example, if they happened to see that kiss at the ballpark tonight, they aren't already on their way here to kill me, right?"

She laughed. "I'm fairly certain they didn't see it, and no, they aren't on their way to kill you. Besides, I'd protect you. No one would even touch you."

"Isn't that my job?"

"Perhaps. However, I want you to know I wouldn't stand idly by if some wild woman—or my brothers—harassed you."

He grinned. "So noted."

Chloe moved closer, moving one knee against his thigh, and leaned her head nearer to his.

"Should we?" he asked her with a grin when she got within inches of his mouth.

Again, exactly like at the ballpark, Chloe didn't answer, just moved in and pressed her lips to his amazing mouth. Deke's arms came up, hugging her tight as the kiss intensified. Before she realized it, she'd straddled his lap to gain a better connection. He didn't seem to mind, just hugged her closer and proceeded to knock her socks into the next county again.

His shirt came off when she pulled it from him, breaking their decadent kiss only long enough to toss it aside before resuming the carnal lip lock.

Deke's hands slid beneath her shirt, but when he didn't remove it in turn, she stripped it off over her head and dropped it on top of his discarded garment.

His gaze went to her cleavage briefly before he grabbed her again, kissing her with even more wicked intent. Chloe loved it. Their tongues danced together in an ancient rhythm as old as time. He was very good at it.

Her insides buzzed, elevating her to an entirely new level of arousal. One she'd never been to before. Now that she was here, she wanted gratification to be the final result.

Chloe didn't know how long the make-out session lasted. In fact, she lost complete track of time until she heard a car pull up outside her house.

Seeing movement outside the window near her porch, she broke the kiss. "Someone's here."

Deke, still cradling her in his arms, fairly leapt off the sofa. Did he think an enemy had tracked them down? Perhaps this was a standard bodyguard reaction to unexpected guests.

The doorbell rang stridently in the quiet, broken only by the sound of each of them breathing a little harder than normal. She slid her feet to the floor and held on to Deke, not wanting to answer the door. Whoever was out there started punching the doorbell repeatedly.

Chloe pushed out a resigned sigh and moved toward the annoying sound.

Deke grabbed her arm, brushing light fingertips over her bare torso and causing a riot of sensation across her midsection. "Maybe you should put your shirt back on before you answer the door."

"Good idea," she said as the bell pealed again and again. Someone was about to get an earful of her fury over being interrupted. Chloe looked at the clothing pile on the sofa, picked his T-shirt up and put it on. She sniffed the collar and sighed in pleasure. "You smell so good."

"I'm glad you think so, but I hope that isn't one of your brothers here to pummel me."

She laughed and shook her head. "I won't let anyone hurt you. I promise."

"That's my job," he said under his breath. Deke, shirtless and drool-worthy, followed her to the door.

Chloe looked through the peephole and stiffened. "What the hell?"

"Who is it?"

"It's Ned. My idiotic blind date from earlier. Can you believe it?"

Deke pushed past her and unlocked the door, putting himself between the opening and Ned with his finger jamming into her doorbell over and over.

"Enough!" Deke shouted. "What do you want?"

Ned stood on the threshold swaying back and forth, obviously drunk off his ass. He took one look at Deke and his bare chest then his glassy stare went past him to gape at Chloe wearing Deke's shirt. "You went home with this loser? And you're fucking him, too?"

Deke stepped into him. "I'm her new bodyguard. Stay away from her or you'll deal with me. Got it?"

Ned stumbled backward when Deke advanced on him. "You can have her. She's a cocktease anyway. Fucking bitch. Your shirt off is as far as you'll go with her tonight, buddy."

Chloe started to launch past Deke to punch Ned one, but her new "bodyguard" stopped her. "Let him go. He's not worth it, right?"

She pressed into Deke's muscular, naked back, taking her focus away from Ned and turning a wide smile on the man she wanted. "Right."

Ned stumbled back to his car, which was parked haphazardly along the curb. The two girls from the stadium were hanging out both curb-side passenger-side windows watching the display as though enjoying an entertaining play.

Deke shut the door, pulled out his phone and made a low-voiced call, watching out the window as he spoke. She didn't hear his words but got the gist he was calling someone to report Ned for his unwanted visit.

Chloe peeked out the nearby window as the woman in the front passenger seat moved over and Ned got in. The woman must be driving. Chloe hoped she was sober. The car pulled away from her house.

Deke checked the deadbolt and turned to her. She slipped her arms around his waist and put the side of her head on his chest, inhaling the same masculine fragrance that tantalized her senses from the shirt she wore.

"Did you call the police?" she asked.

"Not exactly. Just gave information to a friend. I want to make sure he doesn't drive tonight in his condition."

"Okay. Is this friend coming over here?"

"Not that I know of."

"So no one will interrupt us again?"

"Well, can't say that for certain, given the recent visit, but I can promise that no one is coming because of the call I just made."

"Excellent. So can we go back to where we were?"

"If you want to."

"Oh, I demand to."

He laughed and his arms encircled her. She kissed his chest. She kissed his chin. She had to stand on tippy toes to reach his mouth until he lowered his face to meet her lips.

As they kissed, Deke picked her up. She wrapped her legs around his middle like a monkey on a tree. He went back to the sofa exactly where they'd been before being rudely interrupted. She pulled his T-shirt off, easing it up her torso slowly in a short striptease, and deposited it back on the pile where her discarded blouse rested.

"Something else I want you to know," she said quietly.

"What's that?" He put his hands on her bare waist, glancing at her cleavage before looking her in the eyes.

"I'm not a cocktease."

His eyes narrowed. "I already know that. Do I need to go find him again and better defend your honor?"

"No. You need to stay with me tonight so I can prove it to you."

"You don't need to prove anything to me, Chloe. I know what I need to about you." He pulled her close and pressed his mouth to hers, licking between her lips to devour her like she wanted him to. His hands roamed across her back, touching, massaging, caressing. She was lost to it. He stroked his hand down her hair gently a few times as if memorizing its texture and softness level. She wanted him. Wanted him to touch her everywhere.

The skin-to-skin contact intensified their already heated enthusiasm, and shot her up to a completely new height of desire, beating the earlier record breaker.

Fantasies about all manner of decadent things leapt into her mind. The star of these wicked dreams was none other than Deke Langston, her personal bodyguard and top scorer on her private checklist of worthy attributes for the first man in her bed.

What would it feel like if his hands were below her belt? The mere idea sent her mind spinning in several very carnal directions.

She made a decision. Deke was the one. He was absolutely perfect. What was she waiting for?

"Let's go upstairs," she broke their kiss long enough to whisper.

"Upstairs?" he echoed, kissing her again.

"To my bedroom."

"Your bedroom?"

"Are you going to keep repeating whatever I say or come with me?"

He was breathing hard when he answered, "Sorry. All the blood in my head made a hasty trip south the moment we started kissing again. I don't have any brainpower left to answer questions. Besides, that's not what I expected when I came in for coffee tonight." His lips fastened to hers again and his arms tightened as if he couldn't hug her hard enough. "You don't have to prove anything to me."

Straddled over his thighs put Chloe in an excellent position to grind herself down on the body part demanding the extensive blood supply he'd mentioned, which had formed a nice bulge in his lap. He groaned into her mouth and squeezed her harder.

"The thing is, even if you didn't expect it, I really want you." She kissed him quickly before he could respond. "Please come upstairs with me."

Deke grinned. "Tell me. What will happen when we get up there?"

She grinned back. "Let me put it this way—what do you want for breakfast in the morning?" She traced her forefinger from his collarbone, through a sexy sprinkling of chest air to the top of his six-pack, tracing each muscle slowly as she moved lower and lower.

"I want the same thing I suspect I'm about to get for a late-night snack."

"Good answer."

CHAPTER 4

Deke had not expected to spend the night. He was awash in her seductive scent and kissing her for a second round on her sofa made him and his neglected libido light-headed with bliss.

Following Chloe upstairs to her bedroom, his heart pounded a crazy hard rhythm. He wondered if he should do this, but knew he couldn't stop himself if she was determined. And Chloe seemed very determined.

She led him to the door at the end of the short hallway. He'd peeked in earlier to discover it was her bedroom. It smelled like her, but he hadn't entered, feeling like he was trespassing. He wanted to be invited in one day, he just didn't expect it to be tonight, but that also worked.

He planned to stay close anyway, inside or out, after her idiot blind date showed up to harass her. It wasn't always easy for him to turn off bodyguard mode, but right now it was the last thing on his mind.

She dropped his hand and moved to pull the sheets down, kick her shoes off and unbutton her jeans. She turned her back to him and bent over to slide her jeans slowly down her lovely legs before kicking them off. He was riveted by the seductive view of her stripping for him and his mouth went dry staring at her lovely backside.

She wore only a bra designed to entice and very skimpy panties to match. He was entranced and seduced and she hadn't even faced him yet. Her beautiful long dark hair was as silky as he'd imagined it would be. He couldn't wait to bury his face in it again.

Turning slowly to glance over one shoulder, Chloe rotated around, taking her time. Once she faced him, she unfastened her front closure bra, allowing the cups to fall away slightly, teasing him with twin curves of creamy flesh, making his dry mouth water before she moved forward and put her hands on his waist.

Head down, she unbuckled his belt, unbuttoned his jeans and drew his zipper all the way down. Her fingers brushed against his stiff cock through his briefs and it was his turn to tremble with unfettered desire. He wanted so much to please her.

Deke bent down, kissing the top of her head and inhaling her unique scent as she pushed his jeans down to his thighs. He wanted her with a desire he'd never felt before. He wanted this night to be perfect. He already knew he wanted her for more than just this night or he would have begged off and not come upstairs. He didn't believe in one-night stands.

Chloe lifted her face toward his, her expression pensive.

"What are you thinking, Chloe?"

"That I want you so much I'm not sure I can get my limbs to work properly."

Deke smiled and pulled her into his arms. "Me, too." The vast amount of their bare skin touching made him very aware that her limbs were quaking just a little bit.

It had been quite a while since he'd been in such an intimate position. He couldn't even remember the details of the last unmemorable time.

He scissored his legs to make his jeans fall to his ankles. Kicking off his shoes and socks, he stepped from his jeans, grabbed her thighs and lifted her until her legs circled around his waist and then moved to her bedside.

She kissed him for all she was worth as he bent to place her on the bed and follow her down until he was stretched out on top of her. They kissed and kissed, embracing fully, clenched together. Her hips moved against his, their respective parts lining up perfectly. The only thing keeping them apart was a couple of layers of flimsy fabric.

Deke pushed his hips forward in mock sex, pressing his cock hard against the apex of her thighs. She moaned each time they connected. He levered himself onto his elbows and broke the kiss to stare deeply into her eyes. As he rose, one bra cup dislodged, giving him a tantalizing view of bare breast. He pushed out a breath and swooped down to cover her exposed nipple with his mouth, wanting a taste of her.

She arched beneath him as he sucked her tip deeper, moaning, her fingernails digging into his shoulders to keep him in place. He pulled back only long enough to push her bra completely away from the other breast, exposing it for yet another taste. She responded as before, arching, moaning, nails sinking into his shoulder and back.

He wanted this night to be perfect. He wanted to please her. He wanted to lick her. He stiffened as that seductive visual circulated through his head. Releasing her nipple and kissing his way lower, Deke made his way down to where he planned to spend some time getting her ready. When he pulled her panties off, she helped by lifting her hips and pushed out a sigh that sounded like contentment.

Deke kissed her inner thigh once before nuzzling his face between her open legs. The moment he licked her, she sat straight up, a sound of utter shock coming from her lips.

"What are you doing?"

Instead of answering, he licked her again. She groaned a long, tantalizing sound and flattened back onto the bed without further comment. She tasted amazing. Her reaction fanned the flames of his libido to a roaring furnace of desire, so much so he hoped he wouldn't lose it before she climaxed.

It didn't take long. Suddenly her back arched and a breathy shriek came next. He kissed his way back to her breasts, indulging himself as she recovered.

"That was so unbelievably…um…it was good."

He released her nipple and murmured, "What you really mean to say is that it was sexy as hell."

Her trill of laughter washed over his soul with warmth and brought with it more desire. "Yes. And now I want more."

Deke wanted to give her more. "Let me get something out of my wallet."

She pointed to her nightstand. "In the drawer."

He reached out and found an unopened box of condoms. Slipping his briefs off, and securing protection while she watched him like she'd never seen it done before was something else that was sexy as hell.

Deke stared into her eyes the whole time he rolled the condom in place. He climbed back on the bed over her exactly where he'd been before, lowering his hips into the cradle of her welcoming open thighs.

Now the two layers of flimsy fabric were gone. He could take her at any time, but he waited. He knew in his soul that this first time with her was something special. Something to be treasured. Something he'd never, ever forget, regardless of what happened between them in the future.

He kissed her tenderly, pouring his soul into this

connection, wanting her to know how special she already was to him. One of her arms wrapped around his neck, tightening and moving him closer. She kissed him deeper, shifting her hips until he was poised at her slick entrance. Her hand went to his hip, pulling him near in invitation.

Thrusting forward, he breached her slowly, methodically, feeling warm, taut, and then really super tight. He paused, but the hand on his hip urged him deeper inside her excruciatingly wonderful snug heat.

He broke the kiss, wanting to ensure he didn't hurt her. "You feel amazingly tight."

"Do I?" She kissed his chin. "Maybe you're just really big." She kissed his mouth next, but something in her tone gave him pause. She seemed eager, but he thought he detected a hint of unease.

"Am I hurting you?" he asked, stopping his progress halfway inside her incredibly tight body. Wait. Oh no. *Is she...?*

"You aren't hurting me." She shifted her hips upward fast and hard, forcing his cock all the way inside her body in one quick rush of pleasure that required him to focus very carefully so he wouldn't let loose.

Deke trembled on the brink of release, and couldn't believe he was so close after only pushing inside her once. "Please tell me this isn't your first time."

"Sorry, I can't tell you that. Actually, that's a lie. I'm not sorry in the least. My firsts tonight include the limo ride and now the Deke ride." She giggled. "It's a night of perfect and wonderful firsts for me."

She kissed him soundly. He was clenched in her arms as if she were afraid he'd get away. She didn't have to worry. He wasn't going anywhere.

Deke didn't waste time with regret. If she wasn't sorry, who was he to be remorseful? But he did plan to make the night memorable.

He pulled out partway, but she held tight. "Please don't go. Please don't be angry."

Deke smiled and kissed her with tender care. "I'm not angry and I'm not going anywhere. But I really want to move in and out just a little bit, you know?" He pumped his hips a couple of times, barely moving within her because it was as much as she'd let him travel.

She grinned back. "Okay. Move however you want. Hard. Fast. Deep. But keep in mind that I won't break. I promise."

Deke nodded and started out by kissing her hard and fast and deep. He was a little aggressive, but didn't want her to think he wasn't fully invested in tonight's premier activities. He was plenty invested, plenty excited to proceed, and perhaps just a bit flattered she'd chosen him to be her first.

He pulled almost all the way out and slid back inside quickly. She moaned and kissed his jawline, his neck, his shoulder, nipping him once playfully. He liked that a lot.

Deke's thrusts increased, both in depth and in speed. He had a palm secured on the outer part of her thigh for leverage, but as he penetrated her silken body he knew he wouldn't last much longer. He moved a hand between them to stroke her hot spot, wanting to hear her climax again before he leapt over the edge and into what promised to be an endlessly deep pleasure stupor.

She moaned the moment he touched her. Her eyes popped opened, a flash of green watching him in surprise as he continued to rub her.

Five strokes later she stiffened beneath him, screamed something inarticulate, and proceeded to kiss his shoulder and neck repeatedly. After a few more kisses, and to his utter shocked delight, she bit him.

The instant her teeth pressed into his skin with more than just a little intent, he managed one last very deep, hard thrust, and let go with his next breath. It was the most exquisite release he'd ever known. Pleasure raced through his body, through his blood to the very marrow of his bones, every cell replete with utter and complete satisfaction. His thrusts faded even as contentment filled him to the brink of his capacity.

Once his hips stopped moving and settled against her open thighs, he buried his face against her neck and inhaled her sweet scent, imprinting the unique fragrance of this moment directly on his soul.

He kissed her gently once beneath her ear, added another light buss on her cheek, trailed his mouth over her skin, moving to cover her lips with his, tender in the aftermath of shattering ecstasy. She obliged him, a soft sigh escaping her lips before their mouths connected fully.

Deke wanted to say so many things, and also nothing, as if speaking would ruin the quiet moment awash in subtle reflection.

She pulled back slightly. "I can't wait to do that again," she whispered.

"I can't either," he responded, tucking his face next to hers, taking in a few more breaths before having to move. He pressed his mouth to her collarbone.

She stroked her fingertips down his back. "Can I be on top next time?"

"Absolutely," he responded sedately. "In fact, I'll insist on it."

"Good. I've seen it in several movies and television shows, and I've always wanted to try it."

Deke lifted his torso off of her. "We could save it for next time."

Chloe shook her head, frowning. "But what if there isn't a next time?"

"Why? Are you through with me already?"

"No." She laughed, placing a hand on the side of his

face and staring deeply into his eyes. "I just wouldn't expect you to want me—"

"I kissed you back, and I meant it. And this," he nudged his hips subtly against her. "This changes everything. Now you're stuck with me."

"There are worse things."

"Yeah?"

"You know there are. You did rescue me from a stupid Neanderthal, twice in the same night."

Deke laughed. "I should probably send him a fruit basket. If he hadn't been such a jerk, I'd be at home all alone right now. I have to tell you that this is so much better than all alone."

"I agree. All alone totally sucks."

He carefully pulled away from her, seeking the bathroom he'd used before. By the time he returned to the bedroom, knowing what waited for him in round two, his cock had roused enough to be ready to go.

Chloe sat cross-legged in the center of the bed, an unwrapped condom in her hand.

"May I put it on this time?" she asked with a sexy grin.

CHAPTER 5

Chloe's heart rate likely hadn't dipped below two hundred since they'd come upstairs to her bedroom.

"Of course. I'm all yours," he said, joining her on the bed and lying flat on his back for her to do as she pleased.

By the time she'd carefully and slowly rolled the protection into place, his cock had swelled to an impressive girth. "See? Look at you. You're huge."

"It's all for you."

She leaned down to kiss him. His hands had rested behind his head as she'd applied the condom. Now he wrapped his long arms around her shoulders and pulled her tight. When they broke apart, she noticed the red spots on his shoulder.

"Wow. I left teeth marks on you."

Deke reached up to rub the spots. "I didn't mind. But don't forget, next round it's my turn."

She laughed. "It's only fair."

Chloe straddled him slowly, taking in every moment she could to memorize this night for future reference. He didn't seem opposed to seeing her again, but she didn't want to take that for granted. The sexiest love scene in her opinion was when the heroine straddled the hero and rode him enthusiastically to a natural conclusion. Every single time she'd seen it, she vowed to do it the first time she got the chance.

Girl on top, riding her man scenes were always guaranteed to get Chloe's blood up. She wanted to try it more than anything in the world with Deke.

Even after the blazingly sexy round one they'd shared, she almost looked forward to round two more. At last, she could try this long wished for position.

Deke slid his body up toward the headboard, stacking the pillows behind his shoulders as she settled her knees on either side of his hips. She clasped his erection and started to insert him right away, but he stopped her.

"Wait. Let's kiss for a minute. I need some tender loving care before my next performance."

Her lips curved. "Fair enough." He was already hard, but she appreciated that he wasn't in a hurry or ready to get it over with. Chloe inhaled, released her breath slowly and prepared to take her time.

To that end, she leaned forward to capture his mouth in what she'd already discovered was kissing perfection. She'd never in her life been kissed the way Deke kissed her. He bunched the curtain of her hair in one loose fist, rubbing his fingers through the length of it.

Chloe drove her tongue between his lips to ease into the next round. He was right. It was so much better to kiss, lick and touch each other until they couldn't keep themselves from having sex.

He gently cupped her breasts, teasing her nipples with his thumbnails, scraping them across the delicate flesh and driving her crazy with desire until she fairly panted for more.

He was so good at this.

The tingle between her legs had become a rampant, need-filled she-beast ready to take what *she* wanted. It hadn't taken long.

As he played with her, Chloe shifted her hips to take him inside. To possess him. To ride him. She kissed him hard. He kissed her just as hard in return. The tip of his cock teased her slick entrance, promising delights sure to come. Before thinking it through too much, she impaled herself, taking him deeply to his grunt of shocked pleasure.

She probably would have stopped after a few strokes, but he practically growled in approval when she moved harder and faster. Their carnal kiss dissolved into panting and intense staring as she flattened her hands above the headboard on the wall to gain leverage each time she drove her body down on him.

Chloe felt all-powerful. She loved the way his eyes practically rolled back in his head each time she moved over him, taking him deeply within her body and then retreating, only to repeat the action methodically at her own speed.

Each time she moved on him she got a reaction. Before long, he moved his hand between them, rubbing his thumb across her clit, until she rode him faster and faster. Their gaze hadn't broken. He groaned every so often, whether she went up or down. Her arousal built higher and higher until she was practically on the high dive of orgasms to come.

She wanted to take that seductive leap more than anything, but didn't want to surrender or for this exceptional moment to be over. Deke's eyes lowered halfway as if almost gone. He pinched one nipple, continuing his strokes below, each rub more arousing than the last, pushing spasms of pleasure through her body every time he touched her.

Deke smiled all of a sudden, watching her insistent gaze as if he could read her mind and knew how turned on she was, knew how desperately close she was to release.

The climax took her by surprise. She'd been staring into Deke's luscious bedroom brown eyes. He observed her carefully, as if seeking entrance to her very soul with an intensity she'd never experienced.

He overwhelmed her from every level and every direction. His kisses delighted her. His fingers pleasured her. His gaze enthralled her. One last intimate stroke below pushed her over the edge and into volatile rapture.

She shrieked his name, her inner walls squeezing him as her orgasm stunned her senses. His eyelids dipped and a knowing smile encompassed his lips as she came hard. She kept riding him. Each plunge downward to encompass him was ecstasy personified.

One arm surrounded her waist and tightened to a delicious pressure. Whereas before he'd been content to let her ride him at her own speed, suddenly he thrust his hips upward to assist in the gratifying union of their bodies. He buried his face into her neck, kissing along her shoulder.

Three more aggressive strokes and he stiffened beneath her as a low growl escaped his lips. He nipped her shoulder in a subtle little pinch right after his hips stopped moving. Another low growl filled the air as his teeth released her skin. The idea that he wanted to mark her just like she'd marked him sent her heart rate spiraling again.

Chloe's palms slid from the wall above and she slumped on top of Deke, chest heaving with harder breaths than even last time.

"Best sex ever," she managed to say against his chest. She felt the rumble of his laughter.

"You're right. The very best." He rubbed his thumb over the spot he'd nibbled.

"I bit you harder last round."

"I didn't bite you as hard as I wanted to," he said in an amused tone.

"Maybe next time you will."

"Definitely next time I will," he said, pushing out a long sigh that sounded like the very definition of contentment.

Deke wrapped his arms around her and rolled her onto her back before disengaging. He stumbled to the bathroom, leaving her flat-out exhausted and dozing on her bed. She was fairly certain her legs wouldn't work if she tested them.

He came back an undetermined amount of time later. She woke with him seated at her bedside, stroking her face with gentle fingertips.

"What are you doing?" she asked, wondering why he wasn't already snuggled up next to her.

"Watching you sleep."

She lifted up on one elbow. "Why?"

"I wasn't certain you wanted me to spend the night."

"Of course I do. I promised you breakfast." She grinned. "I'm already looking forward to it."

He smiled back. "That's right. I forgot. You distract me."

"Get in bed with me. Let's sleep together."

He kissed her temple. "Oh, I believe we already accomplished that. Twice, in fact, with boundless finesse and so much pleasure I may be ruined."

"Me, too." She sighed deeply, meaning it from the bottom of her heart. First time with Deke and she couldn't imagine ever wanting anyone else.

Deke climbed into bed scooting under the covers. He spooned up behind her, wrapped his arm across her chest, sliding his hand over her opposite shoulder. His chest hair tickled the space between her shoulder blades.

Cocooned together after an amazing evening, Chloe figured she'd sleep like the dead. Thoughts of what position she wanted to try first thing in the morning danced in her head. She smiled to herself, thinking maybe they wouldn't even have to move from their current position.

In the aftermath of the most sublime pleasure he'd ever been part of, Deke dozed on and off, waking each time to discover he hadn't been dreaming. He truly *was* spooned up against Chloe after not one but two rounds of amazing sex. He hadn't been lying when he said he might be ruined for sex with anyone else.

The first round was so unexpected and meaningful he knew he'd remember it for the remainder of his life. The second time was all about her long-sought desires, but equally significant for him, to his way of thinking.

Chloe slept soundly. Her quiet breathing charmed him as much as everything else about her did. Given how they'd spent the last couple of hours, he should be dead to the world, but found he couldn't quite nod off into total sleep. He risked waking her by stroking his fingertips down her arm, off one elbow to her waist and then pressing his palm to her bare hip, just wanting to touch her and stay connected.

She was naked beneath the sheets and her lovely backside was pressed intimately into his very happy lap. He rubbed her hip, and then reached down to stroke her thigh, fingertips dancing along her soft skin and back up to her hip again. She didn't even stir.

It was very satisfying to realize he'd pleasured her into a slumber so deep she didn't rouse when touched or stroked.

Deke smiled to himself, buried his face into the nape of her neck against the softness of her hair, trying to relax and catch a few hours of sleep. They did have a special breakfast planned together. He couldn't wait.

He inhaled again, letting her unique fragrance imprint on his lungs once more, closed his eyes and tried to turn his brain off. If he'd ever been more content he couldn't remember when and it probably wasn't important anyway.

The tinkling sound of breaking glass somewhere in the house made the drowsy, satisfied feeling scurry far away to hide as his ever-present bodyguard mode roared to the forefront in a millisecond. He listened, but heard nothing. Had he only dreamed the noise? Had he even slept yet?

Either way his body was rigid against hers, his senses hyper alert. Then more broken glass sounds reverberated in the night. It sounded like glass was being cleared from a broken pane. He heard the almost inaudible snick of the deadbolt releasing from the direction of the kitchen.

The squeak of a door opening downstairs confirmed he'd heard what he thought he had and prompted his next action. He woke Chloe up. Or rather, he tried to wake her up. She was sleepy and unresponsive.

He whispered, "Chloe!"

"What?" she seemed to ask in her sleep. Her eyelids fluttered. "What's wrong?" But her eyes closed again. He put his arm beneath her shoulders and lifted her halfway up before she stirred completely.

Once he finally got her sitting upright, he whispered urgently, "Where's your cell phone?"

She looked at the nightstand and he followed her gaze. It wasn't there. "Must be downstairs on the coffee table," she muttered, still barely awake. "Why? Who do you need to call?"

The crunching sound of someone walking on glass downstairs floated upstairs. Suddenly wide awake, she sucked in a deep breath of panic and said loudly, "Is someone in the house?"

"Shh." He kissed her gently to calm her. "I think so.

Get dressed. I'll go down and see." He slid from the sheets and stood next to the bed.

"No. Wait." She grabbed his arm and whispered urgently, "Don't go. Please. What if he has a gun or something this time?"

Deke knew she thought Ned had come back. He didn't want to alarm her, but he doubted Ned was the one who'd broken in. The last time someone had broken into his place was years before, and involved some very nasty cartel people. "Maybe it's not your blind date. What if it's a run-of-the-mill burglar?" *Or worse, a vengeful someone from my past, which is littered with the foulest types of human beings imaginable.*

"That's worse." She scrambled out of bed and hugged him close to her naked body, which was difficult to ignore even in full-on bodyguard mode. "Either way, I don't want you to get hurt. Let them take what they want and leave."

"Sorry. Waiting around is not in my nature or my DNA." He disengaged from her carefully, bent down and grabbed his boxer briefs then his jeans, putting them on in a hurry. Their shirts were still downstairs on the sofa. He wished he had a weapon, but figured having surprise on his side was just as powerful.

Pulling his phone from his pocket, he turned it on, punched in the security code and dialed 911. He handed Chloe his cell to relay their accurate location to the operator. He steered her toward the large closet and pushed her inside as she whispered into the phone.

He expected to hear the sound of someone searching for valuables downstairs. Instead, he heard nothing but dead air.

Worried the intruder was headed upstairs, Deke moved toward the door.

"Come here," he commanded in a low tone. Chloe

scrambled out of the closet, phone gripped in her hand and eyes wide with fright.

"Lock this door behind me."

She hesitated, searching his eyes for assurance.

"Do it," he said in a calmer tone that he felt. More glass-crunching sounds came from below.

"Please," he added, softening his tone further. She wasn't one of his clients. He shouldn't order her around like she was paying him.

She nodded. He slipped through the door, closing it behind him. He paused, waiting to hear her slide the flimsy door lock into place. The door opened a crack.

"Deke," she whispered loudly through the slit. "*Please* be careful."

"I will." He winked at her, not sure if she could see in the dimness of the hallway, and pulled the door shut. This time he heard her lock it.

Deke flattened himself along the wall, moved a few steps and bent to get a glimpse of the downstairs. His eyes were fairly well adjusted to the darkness in the hallway. The ambient light from a streetlamp out front cast a handy beam of illumination through a window across the base of her L-shaped staircase.

A figure dressed all in black complete with a ski mask and black gloves rounded the corner from the kitchen and slowly began ascending the stairs. Deke didn't hear a thing, but saw the shape move up and toward him.

Deke hid in a blind spot next to the top step and waited for the intruder to pass. Time ticked by, making him crazy with the desire to chance a look around the corner, but he didn't. He waited, muscles coiled and ready to strike.

The shape of a gun came into view first. Deke let the intruder step up onto the final tread before kicking him solidly in the midsection.

"Oof," the intruder said, his arms windmilling as he struggled to keep his balance. The gun flew out of his hand and over the railing to clatter on the hardwood floor below. He managed to grab the railing on his way down the stairs backward and stopped his own fall. Recovering instantly, he launched forward into Deke's partially hidden space.

They both fell to the floor by the top stair tread. The guy was fairly tall, but Deke had a couple of inches on him. Mostly he was very solid, muscled not fat. Deke managed an elbow to the side of the guy's head. The action resulted in an angry punch to Deke's belly, but at least the guy wasn't on top anymore.

Deke realized quickly the intruder had skills. Plus, he didn't smell like he'd been drinking. Definitely not Chloe's blind date. He'd smelled like a brewery from three paces. Perhaps Ned had sent someone else to bother her this time.

He got onto one knee and shoved the other guy down the first half of the staircase. The intruder ended up on his shoulder on the landing below. He started to follow him down, but the guy gained his feet quickly and headed back up the stairs. He sprinted up the last two steps, butting his head into Deke's side before he was prepared.

Deke crashed sideways into the railing. The momentum of the push left him off balance. A flash of pain like a needle prick followed by a burning sensation in his side made him grunt and sway in the opposite direction. His limbs suddenly felt like melted honey. What the hell?

He momentarily lost his bearings in the dark and unfamiliar terrain.

The intruder shoved him hard and all of a sudden he was airborne, headed over the edge of the railing. It was a short fall. He came down hard on a table, leading with his shoulder, rolled off and landed flat on his back on the wood floors below. He also landed on the gun. The hard metal dug into the back of his thigh.

Deke's whole body ached like a son of a bitch. The burning sensation in his side grew, spreading along his torso like a ring of wildfire on a prairie. He kept his eyes shut, as if that would help absorb and dissipate the impact of the fall along with the scorching puncture wound so he could get up again. It didn't seem to be working. If anything, his limbs felt useless.

He assessed his injuries again, and determined nothing obvious was broken based solely on his pain level. Opening his eyes briefly, he saw the masked guy looking over the rail at him, possibly searching for signs of life. Deke tried to move but his body seemed sluggish and slow to recover.

The intruder descended the stairs in his direction. Deke was panicked to realize he couldn't move, and didn't know why. Had he hurt something serious in his back on the way over the railing or when he hit the table? Was he paralyzed? Whatever the reason, something was very wrong.

Deke opened his eyes again to discover the intruder standing over him. The upside down ski-masked face looked ominous from this position.

Move, body, move! Move now! Nothing.

The guy bent, shoved meaty, gloved hands beneath Deke's shoulders and hooked them under his arms. He started to drag Deke toward the kitchen. The gun lodged beneath Deke's thigh scraped along the wood floor. He could feel it but couldn't move his limbs to recover it. If the intruder heard it, he ignored the gun in favor of his arduous dragging chore.

There was an indistinct noise upstairs. Did a door just open? To his horror, Chloe called out in an overloud whisper, "Deke! What was that crash? Are you okay?"

The intruder's masked face turned up the dark stairs in her direction once before looking down at Deke in the scary upside-down way. The unmistakable smile through the mask hole looked sinister.

He couldn't speak, but he shook his head back and forth in a useless attempt to get this intruder to ignore her. The guy's smile widened. He dropped Deke's arms, allowing his head to knock against the floor, and moved up the stairs. Damn it all to hell.

Deke tried to talk, tried to warn her, but the wind had been knocked out of him. Or worse, he was paralyzed. No voice came when he tried to yell at Chloe to hide. Would he stop breathing next?

A slight buzz of feeling flared in his chest. To his vast relief, he was able to roll his torso back and forth. He couldn't move his legs, but it was as if whatever had paralyzed him earlier was wearing off.

Or he'd hit his head on the way down to the first floor and only imagined this whole scenario, but he didn't think so. His head didn't feel like he'd banged it, but something was definitely wrong.

Either way, with some grit and pain, he was able to move to a sitting position. Unfortunately, it didn't last.

As soon as he was halfway upright, he blacked out.

CHAPTER 6

When Chloe opened her bedroom door and called out to Deke, she realized she couldn't see a damn thing in her hallway. She wanted to turn the hall light on, but was afraid it would make the situation worse.

She heard someone on the stairs and hoped it was Deke. Decided, she flipped the light to the hallway on, prepared to turn it back off again in an instant.

A stranger dressed completely in black was climbing the staircase. He stared at her through the eye cutouts and the mouth hole showed a grim smile of determination. It was scarier than if he'd grinned evilly like a cartoon villain. Stifling a scream, Chloe flipped the light back off and called out again. "Get out! I've called the police. They'll be here any second."

A peek out the door showed the intruder was almost at the top of the stairs and still moving toward her. She closed her door and locked it. The thought of leaving Deke out there alone and possibly hurt made her sick to her stomach. She hated locking herself in, but the intruder was coming. What if Deke was unconscious or dead?

Tears welled up at the thought of Deke's demise, obscuring her already limited vision, which was useless.

She sucked in a breath and tried to calm down. He wasn't dead. She wouldn't waste her time thinking that, but he must be incapacitated.

Every single self-defense lesson from the course she'd taken years ago dried up in her brain like drops of water splashed on a sizzling summer sidewalk.

Acting on instinct, Chloe raced into her bathroom and locked that door, too. She climbed into the tub, closed the shower curtain and squatted down, trying to make herself very small. The idea of the black-masked intruder whipping back the curtain to kill her or worse made her realize she needed a better plan.

A frosted windowpane overlooked her oval bathtub-shower combination. She stared up at the etched design as the proud memory of having it installed moved across her brain. She was prepared to break that custom window and head out onto the gabled roof if need be. But only if she got trapped in here and only if the intruder made it to where she cowered in the bathtub.

The sound of sirens in the distance broke through the quiet filled only with her loud breathing and regret, and gave her the first hope since she'd been awakened so suddenly.

A voice sounded from nearby, tiny and indistinct. She stared at Deke's phone clutched in her hand, and realized the 911 operator was still on the line. She lifted the phone to her ear. "Ma'am. Are you there? Are you okay?"

She whispered, "The intruder is upstairs and headed for my bedroom."

"Can you lock yourself inside?"

"Yes, I already did." She realized she was sobbing. "I'm locked in my master bathroom, but my boyfriend is downstairs. He didn't answer when I called out for him." She cried harder, tears streaming down her face. She desperately hoped Deke wasn't hurt or worse.

The thumping she'd heard earlier sounded like someone taking a header down the stairs. There was an unidentified crash a few moments later from near the same location.

The voice in her ear said calmly, "The police are less than a minute away from your location. Please stay safe behind locked doors."

"Okay." She listened hard, hearing not only her thunderous heartbeat, but the distant sirens closing in. "I hear the sirens."

"Just stay where you are, ma'am. I'll let you know when an officer has cleared the house."

After what seemed like an hour, but probably wasn't that long, someone knocked on her bedroom door.

Whoever it was said her name and identified himself as a police officer. The voice over the phone said, "Officer Brown is outside what he thinks is your bedroom door. He should be calling to you now."

Chloe pulled the curtain aside, furtively searching the small bathroom for the intruder as if she wouldn't have heard someone come through the door.

Fear apparently made her stupid.

No one was there. She climbed out of the tub, unlocked the bathroom door and carefully peeked into her bedroom to make sure no one was there. The officer knocked loudly again identifying himself, telling her the house below was secure.

"Is anyone in there with you, ma'am? Are you all right?" the same voice called from right outside her bedroom.

She slowly opened the door to see a uniformed police officer. Numbly, she registered him ask if she was okay. Nodding, she asked quietly, "Where is Deke?" Not waiting for an answer, she screamed, "Deke! Where are you?"

The officer didn't stop her as she raced past him and

fairly flew down the stairs. Seeing Deke flat on his back at the bottom of the staircase with his eyes closed made her heart shudder. Two paramedics, a man and a woman, were on either side of Deke, one inserting an IV, the other looking in his eyes and then seemingly checking for broken bones.

"What happened to him?" she asked, dropping to her knees at his head. Distractedly, she thought he looked just as gorgeous upside down. She bent over and kissed his forehead, just wanting to connect.

"Looks like he went over the edge and crashed into this side table, which broke his fall," the guy squatted on the right next to Deke said.

"Please tell me he's still alive and breathing."

"He's breathing. Just unconscious," the female paramedic said, putting a stethoscope around her neck after presumably checking Deke's heartbeat.

"Does he have a concussion from the fall?" Chloe asked.

"We couldn't find any contusions on his head. While it's possible that's what's keeping him out, more likely it's this." The guy pulled up a syringe-like device with a short needle from next to Deke's side. "Looks like someone jammed a dose of something into his side."

"What is it?"

He shrugged. "Won't know until it's tested. Possibly a tranquilizer. Or an opiate. No way to know for certain without a blood test. But his pulse is strong and his respiration even, and those are both very good things."

A third paramedic entered her house pushing a portable stretcher.

"How long will he be unconscious?"

The first paramedic shrugged. "Hard to say until we identify what he was shot with. They'll figure it out at the ER. Not to worry. There are no discernable broken bones or any other serious injuries. Just a few bruises and the puncture wound."

Deke was still shirtless. Her gaze darted to the place on his shoulder where she'd bitten him. Heat blazed in her cheeks at the realization they might figure out what that mark was from, and she waited with heart-pounding certainty that they were about to say, "We also think the intruder bit your boyfriend on the shoulder before running off."

"Other than whatever is in the injector and a few bruises from the fall, he's the picture of health."

Chloe was not reassured. She bent over and kissed his forehead again, moving back as they carefully loaded him onto the stretcher.

Deke roused the second he was placed on the litter, alarm filling his expression. "Wait! Stop! What's going on? Where are you taking me? Chloe!"

He tried to sit up, but fell back, eyes dipping closed as he obviously fought to keep them open. In a weaker tone, he asked, "Where is Chloe? Is she okay? Did he get her?"

The paramedic on his right put a hand on Deke's shoulder to keep him down. That only seemed to alarm Deke more.

"Chloe!"

"I'm right here!" She raced to his side, taking his hand in both of hers. "I'm fine. He didn't get me. You'll be fine, too," she said, and hoped she wasn't lying.

Whatever had weakened him appeared to be wearing off, because this time when he tried to sit up, he succeeded. He hugged her tight. "Are you hurt?" He pulled away to stare into her eyes, running his hands down her arms from shoulders to hands. He looked drowsy, like he was still trying to wake up.

"No. I'm perfectly fine. I promise." She smiled, trying to soothe him. He looked relieved. Both paramedics looked like they were long past ready to leave.

Deke sank back on the stretcher. "What's wrong with me? Why can't I keep my eyes open?"

"The intruder might have shot you with a tranquilizer," she said.

"What?" But he put his hand to the exact place on his side where he'd been stabbed with the needle. The nasty-looking puncture mark midway down his side bled a little. "It hurts. He didn't shoot me. He just jammed the syringe into my side when we were fighting."

"Ouch," the EMT guy said. "We should get going to the hospital."

"Can I go with him in the ambulance?" Chloe said.

"Sorry. No room," the female paramedic said.

Deke shook his head, grabbing Chloe's hand. "No. Wait. I can't leave her alone."

"The police will be here for a while longer, right?" the EMT asked a nearby patrolman. The uniformed officer nodded, and added, "Also an investigating detective is on the way to the scene. He'll have some questions for the homeowner."

Deke shook his head. "I don't trust anyone except myself and a very few others for protection."

"I'll watch over her."

Chloe turned toward the speaker and saw an attractive man about Deke's size walk toward them. She'd been so focused on Deke, she hadn't noticed the stranger come into her living room.

"Zak?" Amusement and relief filled Deke's expression. "What are you doing here?"

The paramedics tried to hustle them along, but the newcomer, Zak, gave them such a harsh, chilling look, they backed off. He then turned back to Chloe with a half a smile on his face as if he hadn't just scared the paramedics. Who was this guy?

"I have friends in numerous places. The 911 operator was called using your cell phone, requesting police and an ambulance." Zak smiled mischievously, holding his smart phone up. "I also have a cool new app here, so I was alerted when you called 911."

"Who is this?" Chloe felt a bit nervous. The man Deke called Zak was tall, attractive and very muscular, but he also looked like he belonged in a biker gang.

"Chloe, this is my brother Zak. Zak, this is Chloe."

She nodded. "Nice to meet you. Now that I see you close together, you two *do* look like brothers."

While Deke was a dark and dangerous version of clean cut, his brother looked like a dark and dirty version of a bad boy—hair too long, four days' growth of beard and a faded black leather jacket with well-worn jeans.

Zak grinned, mischief in his gaze. "Oh, yeah? Well, you look exactly like the hot babe I saw in a lip lock with Deke on the kiss cam." She swore his gaze went straight to the bite mark she'd put on Deke's shoulder.

Chloe felt heat rise in her cheeks until they felt ready to burst with embarrassment. "You saw that, huh?"

Zak lifted one shoulder. He nodded, and appeared quite amused by the kiss cam shot and the bite mark, if he'd noticed. Perhaps she was simply paranoid.

"I recorded it." He glanced at Deke, raising his brows as if the footage could be used as a threat.

"Why?" she asked.

"No comment." But he winked, so she assumed it must be brotherly antics at play.

Deke squeezed Chloe's hand. "Listen. There aren't very many people I'd trust with your safety. Luckily, Zak happens to be someone I *do* trust. Even if he recorded that kiss cam shot earlier to blackmail me with our parents." He gave his brother an expressive look as if to say *I know what you're up to,* which Chloe knew was inherent in all sibling relationships, even her own.

She loved that his brother had come here tonight. She promptly dismissed any misgivings about the new scary dude tracking Deke's cell phone calls with an app.

Deke was a bodyguard. Maybe his brother had a similar occupation. Either way, she loved seeing their fond relationship firsthand.

Zak said, "Aw. That's so sweet, bro. And that video means the next time you have home game baseball tickets, I get them, doesn't it?"

The two paramedics were antsy, wanting to get going.

"No promises." Deke tugged Chloe down to kiss her cheek and let the EMTs roll him away to the ambulance. He must be truly drugged up, because she suspected if he could have leapt off the gurney to walk, he would have.

Chloe turned to Zak. "We're going to follow them to the hospital, right?"

"Sure." But then he did a quick head to toes survey of her and asked, "Do you want to maybe put on something other than that?"

"What?" She looked down and realized she only wore the peach silk robe she'd grabbed after Deke stuffed her in the closet. Her selection was a very sheer summer fabric that while fairly secure below the belt, showcased her lack of clothing, because the front gaped open, only barely covering her bare breasts. Face going chili pepper hot, Chloe nodded, snapping the top of her robe closed. "Yes. Good call. I just need a minute to change."

"Take your time."

Before she could scamper off to put more modest clothing on, one of the police officers walked up to the two of them. "Looks like the suspect broke a window in the kitchen door to unlock the deadbolt. Do you have a security system?"

"No. I never thought I needed one in this neighborhood."

The officer gave her a faintly disapproving look and then mentioned that the investigating detective was on his way in to question her. "Once we finish collecting evidence, I'll have one of the techs secure a piece of cardboard over the window for the time being."

"Thank you," she said sincerely. "How long do you think you'll be here?"

He shrugged. "Hard to say," he said. His gaze moved to over her shoulder as if something had caught his attention.

Behind her, Chloe heard a new voice. "Ms. Wakefield?" She spun around and nodded once at the new arrival.

A man with short black hair, dressed in a nice gray suit with a subdued blue tie held up his detective identification for her perusal. She glanced at it, nodded once. Zak also leaned in and took a very long careful look at the detective's credentials.

"I'm Detective Pullman, are you the owner?" he asked, stuffing his ID back into his side pocket once Zak had given it a thorough examination.

Chloe nodded, resisting the sincere urge to dance back and forth on the balls of her feet like she was standing on a blazing, hot sidewalk. She wished she wore more than just a robe for the coming discussion. "Yes. I am."

Detective Pullman gave Zak a quick once over look, and asked, "Are you also an owner here?"

Zak looked amused. "No. I'm not." But didn't explain why he was there.

"He's Deke's brother," Chloe said, by way of clarification. "You know, my friend who was taken to the hospital already."

The detective nodded, but didn't respond or make note.

"We did an initial test swab of the syringe used on your friend, which tested positive for opiates. They'll do a more thorough test at the hospital for a full work up."

Pullman then asked Chloe for her account of what happened. As concisely as she could, Chloe told him everything that happened, even mentioning the earlier disruption when Ned stopped by unexpectedly, but not the whole story of the blind date or the baseball game.

Zak steadfastly remained by her side, hands shoved in the pockets of his leather jacket, not saying a single word during her account or Pullman's further questions.

An officer stopped briefly to say the upstairs had already been processed. Pullman nodded and asked a couple more questions before releasing her to follow Deke to the hospital.

There were still several tech people milling around her kitchen and living room, but Chloe wanted to get upstairs and finally change clothes.

"Care if I look around a little bit?" Zak asked politely, but looked like he'd do whatever he wanted regardless of her answer. Besides, the tech people still collecting evidence would likely keep him in line.

"No. Go ahead. Make yourself at home. I'll hurry and get dressed."

"Do you still have my brother's phone by chance?"

"Yes." She pulled it from the pocket of her robe. The screen had gone blank. She handed it to Zak. "I don't know the lock code to open it."

"I do," Zak said in an amused tone and started pushing buttons. "Go get dressed, okay? We'll leave as soon as you're ready."

"I'm sorry."

That got his undivided attention. His intense gaze went straight to her eyes. "For what?"

Tears welled up before she could stop them and Deke's brother got that panicked, uncomfortable look all men get when faced with a female crying for unclear reasons.

"Deke made me lock myself in my bedroom. I should have come out and helped him."

"No. You shouldn't have." Zak pocketed Deke's phone and grabbed her hand, holding it between his rough palms. "Listen. I know my brother. If you'd come down, it would have been worse. He'd have shifted his attention off the intruder and focused on protecting you. He's a bodyguard first and foremost. He locked you in that room so he could do what he does best."

"What's that?"

"Kick ass."

"But he got hurt."

"Because the intruder didn't play fair, stabbing him with some unknown opiate concoction and knocking him on his ass. No one would have been prepared for that. Most importantly, you are not responsible." He patted the top of her hand and gestured for her to go upstairs. "It's going to be okay. Deke will be okay. Get dressed. We'll go straight to the hospital. I expect Deke to be ready to bolt out of there by the time we arrive, if they haven't strapped him down for his own good."

Chloe nodded and trudged slowly up the stairs, face down in dejection. She still felt like she should have tried to help Deke instead of cowering in the bathtub like, well, a coward.

She heard Zak talking to someone in a low tone below. She couldn't make out the words he said, assuming he was calling his family about Deke.

On the top step, she paused. There was something on the floor by the railing. She hadn't seen it until her toe brushed against it because the color had blended in with her carpet runner.

She scooped up what she thought was a crumpled

piece of paper. No, a bent business card. She unfolded it, and froze as she read the name emblazoned at the top of the card.

Justine Keller-Howe. Real Estate Broker. Premier Housing.

CHAPTER 7

Deke wasn't uncooperative, but figured he was the only one in his hospital room who felt that way. He hated even visiting hospitals, let alone being admitted to one as a patient.

It was mental agony being poked and prodded by an endless stream of nurses and interns asking the same damn questions over and over again, which started anew every time someone else entered the room.

It wasn't like he was going to give them different answers after the eleventh or twelfth time they made the same queries. Besides, if he did take a stand and begin spouting misinformation, they'd probably start over. He didn't want to go another ten rounds, so he played their game and repeated himself.

Once the feeling had come back in his legs, he'd swung them over the side of his bed. But the steely eyed nurse attending him, glared without speaking until he'd slipped his legs back beneath the sheet.

They'd probably shackle him to the bed like a prisoner if he failed to cooperate, he thought fancifully. He didn't have his phone, making him feel even more isolated. And where the hell was Zak with Chloe? Weren't they supposed to follow him to the hospital? How long had he been here? It seemed like hours.

Detective Pullman had stopped by for a few minutes to ask about the incident at Chloe's home. Deke hadn't minded answering his questions, since he didn't repeat the same ones over and over again. Plus, he was in and out in a matter of minutes.

A new person in a white lab coat entered the room, carrying a digital pad of some sort. The name Dr. Wishek was stitched on his lapel. The tablet was a modern version of the clipboard with all Deke's repeated information available at the touch of a finger—if anyone had bothered to enter anything he said in any computer system since he'd been here.

"What seems to be the problem?"

"Nothing. I'm fine. Let me go home," Deke said.

The doctor continued his observations as if Deke hadn't spoken. That was nothing new. It wasn't like anyone was actually listening to or recording anything he said. "It says here you were stabbed with a tranquilizer needle and fell over a stair rail." *Yeah. I have the rock star of injuries.*

"Yep."

The doctor hadn't looked him in the eye yet. Deke exhaled slowly, fighting the urge to cause havoc. If he thought it would get him thrown out of this place, he'd do it. He was not going to be a good patient if they required he stay here much longer.

"Any allergies that you know of?"

Seriously? This shit again? "No." *For the hundredth time, but I seem to be developing an allergy to repeating answers endlessly, and I swear if you ask me about any childhood traumas again, I'm going to knock that tablet out of your hands and hold you hostage until I'm freed.*

"Well, wait. I *was* thrown off a staircase from halfway up. I might be allergic to gravity," he said, unable to resist. The doctor continued to stare at the pad, tapping the screen seemingly at random. He was probably playing Candy Crush.

Deke had a sudden flashback of landing on the intruder's gun. No one had mentioned *that* in the endless litany of questions. Detective Pullman hadn't asked either. Deke had forgotten until now. He reached down and rubbed a spot beneath his thigh where a tender patch of skin revealed he hadn't dreamed it.

What had happened to that gun? Surely it would have been noticed on the floor when they lifted him onto the gurney. Chloe hadn't mentioned it. Neither had Zak. Did the police have it? *Fuck.* He needed to get out of this hospital. He wanted to investigate and get some answers. He needed to get released soon. Now.

First on the agenda, he wanted to find Chloe, wrap her in his arms and protect her. His thoughts naturally went back to the scariest former case he'd ever participated in. Cartel thugs had been after him for saving someone they'd wanted dead. He'd thrown himself in front of that guy on three different occasions to keep him alive. They'd kept coming.

"That's funny," the doctor said without a shred of amusement in his tone, ripping Deke's attention away from his uncomfortable past. "Allergic to gravity." He continued staring at the tablet, occasionally poking the screen with his finger.

Before Deke could follow through with his new plan to kick the tablet out of the doctor's hands for being an unfeeling robot, he heard the door beyond the curtained area whoosh open.

Zak poked his head around the curtain's edge, surveyed the situation with a single glance, and ducked back out. Chloe, followed closely by Zak, came through the curtains a heartbeat later.

Ignoring the doctor, Chloe rushed to Deke's side,

kissed his cheek and grabbed his hand. "How are you feeling?"

"So much better now that you're here." Deke squeezed her fingers. "In fact, I'm ready to leave." *If there's time once the doctor finally gets a sugar crush and moves on to the next level of the game he's playing, of course.*

Zak's brows furrowed as he looked over the doctor's shoulder and read whatever was on the tablet. Or he was watching the other man attain a new highest score, beating all of his Candy Crush friends.

"What's the verdict?" Zak asked, moving away. "Is my brother going to live, or do the rest of us get to divvy up all of his stuff?"

The doctor finally stopped tapping on the flat device, looked Deke in the eye and said, "You have a few contusions but no broken bones and no concussion. The time you were unconscious was certainly from the mystery tranquilizer, opiate drug introduced into your system and not a head injury. And it's also the more serious issue."

"Tranquilizer?" Zak asked.

"Yes. As near as we can determine, the substance is a synthetically engineered hybrid opiate tranquilizer drug. Your blood tests were put at the top of the queue, since it was an unknown substance. The largest part of it was a common paralytic and the rest was obviously a very powerful sedative along with some opiates mixed in, but the lab is not sure of its exact makeup or origin. The effects began almost immediately once introduced into your system."

"That's right. I couldn't move once I hit the ground, and then I was knocked out when I tried to sit up."

The doctor nodded. "Although this drug was fast acting and the bulk of it has likely already passed through your system, some may have been stored in your tissues. You may have bouts of weakness in the coming days until it's completely gone."

"So I can leave?"

Instead of answering, the doctor looked at Chloe. "Is this your wife?"

Chloe shook her head and her cheeks went pink.

"Not yet." Zak's grin said the kiss cam video was on his mind.

The doctor continued. "Due to the nature of the drug being a mystery design and manufacture, I'm unsure of all the side-effects you may experience. Therefore, I'm recommending bed rest for three days minimum and absolutely no driving. Also drink plenty of water. It will help flush out any residual drugs. It would be a good idea for you to see your regular doctor at that point for more blood work, just to confirm the drug is gone."

"Three days of bed rest? Unlikely," Deke said under his breath. But at least the doctor wasn't ignoring him anymore.

"Also, it would be best if *someone* stayed with you for the next forty-eight hours, and seventy-two hours would be better, to ensure there are no further unexpected symptoms or side-effects."

"I can stay with you," Chloe volunteered. She laced her fingers with his and squeezed his hand. She looked into his eyes. "I mean, if you want me to."

"I do." Deke felt a big grin slide onto his face.

"Those two words can get you into trouble, bro," Zak said under his breath, yet still loud enough for them to hear him. Chloe didn't say anything but looked amused.

The doctor left the room with a promise to send a nurse to remove his IV and bring his discharge paperwork.

Deke turned to his brother, lowered his tone and asked, "Did the police find the gun?"

"What gun?"

"The intruder's gun. I kicked it out of his hand and then landed on it when I hit the bottom floor. Did the authorities recover it or did he?"

"I'll check, but I'm fairly certain no one said anything about finding a weapon. All I have is your phone, which I got from Chloe." He pulled it out of his pocket and put it on the table next to the bed.

Chloe put a hand on Deke's arm. "I found something on the upstairs landing after the police finished with the second floor. I know I should give it over to whoever is investigating the case, but Detective Pullman was already gone and I wanted to show it to you first."

She pulled a plastic sandwich baggie out of her purse and handed it to him.

He quickly scanned the wrinkled paper through the plastic. "Isn't Premier Housing where you work?"

"Justine is my boss. Well, she's the broker at Premier Housing. She's the one who set me up with Ned earlier in the evening."

"Who's Ned?" Zak asked. "I heard you mention him to Pullman, earlier."

"Ned was her date to the baseball game."

Chloe sighed. "Maybe Ned sent the man who drugged you. Or maybe it was Justine, though I can't imagine why. Otherwise, why did an intruder have her card?"

Deke handed the baggie to Zak. He gave it a cursory look and asked, "Are you sure the intruder dropped it? I assume you have easy access to your boss's business cards, right?"

"Sure. But it wasn't there when—" she stopped talking and her cheeks turned pink again.

"When what?" Zak asked, sliding an amused gaze to his brother.

Deke answered. "It wasn't there when we went upstairs earlier in the evening."

Zak grinned again. "Okay. But the intruder having this card doesn't mean your boss, or Ned gave it to him. He could have it for another reason. Like maybe our criminal is looking to buy a house with his ill-gotten gains."

"That's a pretty big coincidence, though. Also suspicious, right?"

Zak nodded, but asked, "So was Ned inside your house earlier? Maybe he dropped it when he picked you up for your date."

Chloe frowned. "No. He pulled up to my front door and honked repeatedly until I came outside."

"What a dick move." Zak shook his head.

"One of the many reasons I brought your brother home with me instead."

"He's so lucky, my brother. Great baseball game seats—that he should have given to me—and a kiss cam chance with a hot babe, just to name a couple things. He doesn't deserve his amazing luck, you know."

"But if you'd been at the game instead of Deke, I'm guessing you wouldn't have rescued me from my vile blind date or kissed me or even shared your popcorn."

"Rescued you? Not sure. No kiss? That's absolutely true. My wife really frowns on me kissing other women. Hard to blame her. And the popcorn?" Zak shrugged. "There's no way I would have shared. I really like popcorn." He winked at Deke. "He's lucky and he shares."

The nurse arrived. She was fast, efficient and had Deke out of the hospital room in no time.

He exited the hospital holding Chloe's hand. Zak led them in the direction of several motorcycles lined up along the curb.

He stopped. "Please tell me you did *not* force Chloe to ride on your motorcycle."

Zak held up a key fob, pushed the button and lit up the brake lights of a car parked next to the bikes.

"No. I brought her in my ball and chain's car. I mean, Kaitlin's ride."

Deke laughed. "I'm going to tell your wife you said that."

"No you won't or I send that kiss cam footage to Mom and Dad."

CHAPTER 8

Chloe loved hearing the brotherly banter between Deke and Zak. It was obvious they'd kill or die for one another and it reminded her of the way her brothers ribbed each other during family gatherings.

"Why is sending the kiss cam footage a threat?" she asked.

"Deke doesn't think his job is conducive to relationships. Our parents have given up hope that he'll ever settle down."

"Shut it," Deke said.

"Being a bodyguard isn't conducive to relationships?" Her puzzled gaze shifted to Deke. "Why?"

"You told her what your job is?" Zak asked as if it were some state secret.

"Shut it, Zak," Deke said again. He opened the front passenger car door for Chloe, but didn't answer either of their questions. He motioned her to get in front.

She shook her head. "I'll ride in back. You ride up front with your brother." She grinned. Deke opened the back passenger door for her instead.

"Thanks, Chloe." Zak winked at her. "I love getting good gossip firsthand. I can't wait until our next family gathering."

Deke rolled his eyes and closed her door once she was seated in the back of Zak's wife's ride. He rode in front with his brother. Their light-hearted sparring continued all the way to her home.

The teasing was familiar and comforting, especially after a long night of ultimate and incredible joy directly followed by off-the-charts fright.

Dawn was breaking as Zak dropped them off at Chloe's house. She installed Deke in her bed, cleaned up the broken glass from her kitchen floor and called a repairman to fix the back door, setting up an appointment for that afternoon.

This was not the plan she had for her Saturday, but at least there was an awesome man in her bed. Chloe climbed in with Deke and snuggled next to him. She dozed off quickly, having barely slept at all the night before. She woke an undetermined amount of time later to the smell of bacon frying.

Who was cooking bacon? She stretched, reaching out to where Deke had lain to find an empty space. He wasn't there. She opened her eyes, sat up in bed, and realized she was alone.

Memories from last night's break-in flooded back into her brain with a vengeance. She scrambled out of bed. Unless someone had broken in again, Deke was downstairs cooking.

She snagged her slinky peach robe because it was handy, shoved her arms in the sleeves as she walked and headed downstairs.

Rounding the corner into her kitchen, Chloe stopped at the sight before her. Shirtless and with his jeans slung low on his hips, Deke tended not one but two pans on her stove. One had bacon sizzling and the other looked like it held buttery scrambled eggs. He'd brewed a pot of coffee and set the table, even including small glasses of orange juice. The room smelled heavenly and he looked like an archangel moving comfortably in this arena. A shirtless, sexy archangel.

The toaster popped up two pieces of browned perfection. He transferred the toast from the twin maws of the steaming kitchen appliance to a ready plate and buttered it with an efficient grace she appreciated.

The words *and he cooks* blazed across her mind. He turned with the plate of toast in hand, and grinned as he saw her staring. His bare chest distracted her for only another moment.

She saw a colorful bruise on one shoulder, on the opposite side of where she'd marked him with her teeth, and a white square bandage taped to the place where he'd been jabbed with the needle.

"Hungry?" he asked. She glanced at his abs once more and nodded, unable to speak without drool coming along for a ride.

"Have a seat. It's almost ready."

"You didn't have to cook."

"That's okay. I couldn't sleep."

"You must think I'm a terrible nurse, making you prepare your own food while I sleep in. Especially since I promised to make breakfast for you this morning after luring you up to my bedroom last night."

"Well, the evening took a different turn than expected. I'm rolling with it." He turned back to flip the bacon over. "Besides, a fast and easy breakfast was the least I could do since you volunteered to take me in and watch over me."

"How are you feeling?" Her gaze trailed to that pale square gracing his side.

"I'm fine. Don't worry."

The food might have been simple, but it was delicious and prepared perfectly. In between bites of what had to be called lunch since it was the noon hour, they discussed innocuous topics, avoiding any talk of blind dates, her back door with the hastily applied piece of cardboard box taped over the open pane, or his injuries.

Her phone rang, disrupting their quiet, intimate brunch. The number on the display made her frown. Justine. Crap.

On the final ring before it went to voicemail, Chloe answered, "Hello." Her tone was civil, but only barely. Justine didn't seem to notice.

Her boss had a loud, distinct voice. Currently it was set to harsh, grating bitch tone, jarring Chloe from the lovely discussion she'd just had with Deke regarding favorite foods, favorite movies and many other favorite things.

"What in the ever-loving hell happened last night, Chloe?"

"I could ask you the exact same thing."

The other woman continued as if Chloe hadn't spoken. "Ned is completely pissed. He called me after midnight, screaming about what you did to him."

"Well, he doesn't deserve to be angry. He was the problem, not me."

"He said you ignored him completely on your date and then went home with some stranger you met at the game. Is that true? What were you thinking?"

Chloe loved how Justine had already assigned blame before hearing her side of the story. "Ned told me you guaranteed that I was a sure thing. The first thing he asked me at the game was what I wanted for breakfast. Did you tell him that, Justine? Did you tell him I would have sex with him last night?"

"What?" There was a long, long pause. "Well, no. Not exactly."

"Justine!"

"He's a great client, an entrepreneur, and a self-made

man. He expressed an interest in you. I just wanted you to have a good time. You could do worse."

"That's so wildly mistaken you should have 'liar' tattooed on your forehead! Trust me when I tell you, Ned is the worst. I've already done better." She shot a glance at Deke and he winked.

Justine sucked in a shocked breath. "So it's true. You *did* go home with some other guy after Ned spent all that money on those tickets."

"Yes. Especially after Ned told me to find my own way home because I refused to screw him. I had to find another way back to my house, didn't I?" Ned had told her to find her own way home because she'd kissed Deke, but that was beside the point. He'd been unbearable since the moment he honked repeatedly outside her house to get her to come out. That should have been her first clue as to his character.

"You've made a mistake, Chloe. Ned is powerful in our business. I hope you're ready to apologize to him."

Chloe stood up from her chair, fury coating her every move. "I will never, repeat, *never* say I'm sorry to that Neanderthal. He came to my house unannounced after the game last night, stinking drunk. He rang the doorbell incessantly and when I answered he called me a cocktease. Did he tell you that?"

Deke also stood, and whispered in her other ear, "Don't say anything about the intruder. We don't know who that was."

She nodded her understanding.

Justine said suddenly in her ear, "Wait a minute. Don't you have an open house today at the Sierra Estates subdivision?"

"No. It's tomorrow. And you may have to take it for me anyway. I'm taking care of a sick friend right now."

"That's unacceptable, Chloe. I thought you were a professional."

"I am. That's why I'm trying to get you to cover for me. Besides, after last night's horrid date with Ned, you owe me."

"That is very much in dispute as far as I'm concerned. If you can't make it to that open house tomorrow, we may have to have a serious discussion about your continued association with my brokerage."

"Fine. Bring it. Maybe I don't want to work with someone who'd set me up on a date with a loser like Ned just to make *him* happy."

"Chloe—" Justine's voice had morphed into a fake conciliatory tone. The one she used only for difficult and unreasonable clients.

"Don't, Justine! Don't try to make him sound like a gift. He was vile and he took me to a crowded baseball game, knowing I don't like mobs of people. Besides, I'm not a prostitute that you can pimp out to further your business. Tell me, do we sell houses or sex, Justine? I may have to update my personal business strategy."

Justine pushed out a long-suffering sigh. "I just wanted you to have some fun." But her voice held an edge, sounding a lot like she was more concerned about Ned than anything else. Chloe had been used as a sacrificial lamb to further Justine's aspirations of upward mobility in some unexplained way.

"No. You wanted to have Ned owe you at my expense. I refuse to be treated that way. Change the subject. I'm not going to apologize or discuss him further."

"Fine. Are you going to that open house tomorrow?"

Chloe paused and glanced at Deke. He looked amazing. But she felt like it was her fault he'd gotten hurt. He wasn't supposed to drive and she'd volunteered to look after him. In this moment, taking care of Deke took precedence over her career.

"No. I have something more important to do. Besides, you sacrificed me to a client."

"That's debatable."

Deke got her attention, mouthing that he'd be okay if she had to work. Chloe shook her head.

"Not to me."

Justine pushed out another long breath, but this one sounded as if she'd run out of steam. "Okay. Look. I don't want to fight with you. Let's call this even. I'll cover your open house tomorrow. But I need you to consider at least speaking to Ned. I can't lose him as a client, Chloe. I just can't."

"No promises." It was the only civil thing she could think to say. "I'll talk to you in a few days."

Justine hung up without saying another word. So be it.

Chloe didn't have to remain with Premier Housing. Eventually, she'd planned to go out on her own anyway. Perhaps that far-off vision for her future would come true sooner rather than later.

"You don't have to cancel your open house because of me."

"I know. I did it more because of the break in. I still have to fetch a copy of the police report and call my insurance, and a hundred other things that will come up because of it."

"I'm sorry."

"Don't be. What if you hadn't been here to save me when he broke in?"

"I didn't do much except fall on your floor into a heap of uselessness."

"Not true. You rescued me for a third time in the same night and as a surprise bonus, you made me breakfast."

A bone-melting grin surfaced on his stubble-shadowed face. So sexy. He motioned her closer.

Chloe walked over as he scooted his chair out and gestured for her to sit on his lap. She gently seated herself on his firm legs, leaning in for a quick kiss as she snuggled against his chest. He wrapped his arms round her, nuzzling his unshaved face against her cheek. She palmed his jaw as a naughty vision of Deke's scratchy bearded face lodged between her thighs thrilled her libido.

Sex was likely out of the question, although the doctor had only said Deke couldn't *drive* because of the possible side-effects of the mystery sedative he'd been given.

A vibration beneath her leg startled her off Deke's lap. He hooked his arm around her waist and pulled her back down. "It's just my phone," he said, retrieving it from his pocket and answering with a curt, "Yes."

He kissed her shoulder, which she felt all the way through her slinky peach robe as if she was naked. His whiskers fascinated her.

He stopped kissing and parked his chin on her. "Okay. Thanks for checking, Zak," he said and hung up.

"What did your brother have to say?"

"Not much that's helpful, I'm sorry to report. The intruder must have taken his gun with him before leaving. The police made no mention in their reports of a weapon retrieved at the scene.

"There were also no prints or DNA on the business card except for yours, so he handed it over to the police, telling them you found it after they left last night."

"How did Zak have it tested?" Chloe asked. Deke's brother looked like a dark and dangerous archangel. She hadn't expected him to have the means to do all he'd done.

Deke smiled. "Zak works for a very well equipped private security firm with seemingly endless resources. Your prints must already be in the system. Were you in the military or something?"

"No. My parents had mine registered when I was a teenager in case I was ever kidnapped. It made them feel better." She shrugged. "I still think it could be Ned," she said to change the subject from her parents.

"Unfortunately, Zak said Ned had an alibi for the time in question."

"That doesn't mean he didn't send someone else."

"True. Zak said he'd check a few more places. The only good news he mentioned is that there's no local chatter on the streets indicating it was a gang-related robbery, but I already suspected the intruder was privately hired."

"Why?"

"The way he fought. He was fairly well trained. Initially I thought he was either a burglar looking for some quick valuables or some lowlife Ned hired to scare you. The intruder anticipated my moves once I attacked. I won't underestimate him the next time."

"I'm not sure what worries me more. The idea you think there will be a next time or that it's someone who was skilled enough that you don't want to underestimate him should he try again."

"That's the other thing."

"What?"

"I'm unsure what the intruder's goal was. I know he wasn't here to rob you. If he came to hurt you, he missed a premium opportunity after I was down for the count."

"He must have heard the sirens."

Deke shrugged. "Unfortunately, if he's the trained operative I suspect he is based on his fighting skills, even with impending sirens he would have had plenty of time to get to you if he wanted to."

"So what should we do?"

"We should move you into my place today."

Whoa. What?

CHAPTER 9

"What?" Her surprise might have bothered him, but the way her eyes flared to life at the idea of moving in with him made up for it. Maybe she was only surprised he offered.

Deep in the back part of his brain a voice reminded him of something he tried not to believe. *You're going to get her killed if you remain in her life. The cartel doesn't abduct, they annihilate.* He'd been assured repeatedly that the cartel he'd tangled with was defunct, no longer a viable entity. What if they'd only gone to ground? What if they were back with new resources and retribution on their minds? What if he was once more a target and now, by association, so was Chloe?

Regardless of the imaginary devil on his shoulder spouting horror, hell and damnation, Deke couldn't back away from her. He needed to protect Chloe and he could do a better job of that on his home turf behind the safety of his premium security system.

"I'd like for you to stay with me. I can keep a better eye on you that way."

"Well, I do like it when you pay attention to me."

"Excellent. When can we leave?"

"I can put off the police report and my insurance until

Monday, but I still have to get my back door fixed. The guy is coming this afternoon." She glanced at the clock on the stove. "Look at the time. He'll be here in two hours. I'm a little off my game with my extended morning nap."

"That's what happens when you stay up all night visiting a beat-up guy in the hospital." He brushed his hand down her hair, scratching the center of her back through the very sheer fabric of her robe. Goosebumps rose along her bare arms as he touched her, which satisfied him in a purely primal way.

"Are you okay leaving your house?"

She pondered his question for a moment. He scratched lower down her back. The fabric was soft and sheer and he really wanted to pull the sexy robe off of her and take her on the kitchen table. He'd enjoy hearing the shrieking echo of his name bouncing off the kitchen walls from the pleasure he'd ensure she had.

"I don't want anyone to break in again, obviously, but if they do, I'd rather be at your house instead of waiting here like I was too stupid to live."

He grinned at the reference. "Good. Let's go now. I can get Zak to supervise your door repair and bring your key by my place later."

Chloe nodded after three seconds. "Okay."

She packed a bag with enough clothes to last a week, including a few work outfits. She then drove his sports car back to his house without making him want to close his eyes for the ride.

Zak, on the other hand, drove like a bat out of hell no matter what vehicle he was driving. Whether on a motorcycle, in a car or on a boat, he pushed whatever engine it had to the limits. If his brother ever acquired a pilot's license the world would have to learn to duck whenever he zoomed by. He gave his brother lots of crap, but loved him and all of his family beyond words.

Chloe parked in the center available slot of his four-car garage. An SUV was parked in the fourth spot. Deke pushed the button on the wall to close the door, cocooning them in semi-darkness.

"I can't wait to see inside this house."

"Why?"

She looked sideways then upward as if trying to hide something. "Let's call it professional intrigue."

"What?"

Her expression was suddenly guarded. "I'm a Realtor. I love looking at any and all houses. I feel a little guilty for knowing what I already do about this place."

He retrieved her two bags from his car's very small trunk. "Oh, yeah? What do you know?"

"I know you bought it two years ago and what you paid for it, because I used the amount in my compilation to set the asking price on your neighbor's house down the street," she said very quickly.

He opened the door leading to his kitchen via his laundry room. "So in your professional opinion, did I pay too much back then?"

She shook her head. "Oh no, you got a great deal." She shrugged quickly, shooting him an excited look as she crossed the threshold. He watched her as she assessed his home from her first step inside. She was cataloging it for future reference in the way Realtors did for viability of sale, but she also looked very happy to see it because it was his.

He hoped she liked it, because he loved it. It was a place he'd settled down in after a fairly successful career. When he'd walked in the front door the first time, it felt like home. Or perhaps sanctuary was a better description.

Deke had been sitting on the sidelines after a few particularly harrowing bodyguard assignments in a row.

In fact, the baseball game was the first time in months he'd actually taken a case. And third bodyguard to Garrick hardly deserved the word "case."

He'd been pondering of late if he had his heart in his job anymore. He'd considered taking a job with Zak's place of employment, The Organization, which sounded more ominous than it was. A well-funded private security firm versus renewing his own one-man show bodyguard business—there were plusses and minuses on both sides. He hadn't determined which side the scale fell on harder just yet.

If he agreed to work for The Organization, he could be even less emotionally involved in the cases he'd be assigned. That would have been handy two cases ago. Plus, he'd have unlimited protection and resources if the cartel he'd tangled with wasn't dead and gone like he'd been assured.

"Wow!" Chloe said as she walked into his kitchen. Her zeal distracted him from his dire musings. He loved his house, but had a particular affection for his kitchen. "I can't wait to make you breakfast in here," she said, clapping her hands together and spinning around, seemingly trying to see everything at once.

"You're welcome to cook in here anytime you want."

She ambled out of the kitchen and into the foyer by his grand double door entry. Chloe put her back against the front doors and stared at the first view he'd seen of his place.

"This is spectacular, Deke."

"Thanks. I'm glad you like it."

A wide, circular staircase on the left led to a bridge-like balcony overlooking not only the foyer where she stood, but also the great room. He knew she could also see the comfortable leather furniture and a nice two-story window view to the backyard on either side of the floor to ceiling fireplace. Outside was a pool he never used and an in-ground hot tub he used incessantly. It was a household feature he never wanted to live without.

"Is that a kidney shaped pool *and* an in-ground hot tub?"

"Yes."

Chloe placed a hand over her chest as a sigh of contentment escaped her lips. "Perfect."

They strolled outside to take a closer look.

"Want to get wet with me?" he asked suggestively.

"I didn't bring a suit."

He laughed. "You won't need one." He pointed to the backyard fence that protected his yard. There were no rear neighbors. Instead, his property sloped down a hill, ending at the edge of a golf course in the distance. The only way to see anything in Deke's backyard was to hover in a helicopter, which she knew was not allowed commercially in this area.

The folding room divider made of woven lattice surrounding the hot tub gave a bit of privacy, but not one hundred percent. "Or if you're still shy, I'll loan you another T-shirt."

Color came to her cheeks immediately. He loved that she blushed whenever anything sexual came up. She'd given him her virginity, so perhaps the instinct to blush would fade the more experienced she got. But he hoped not.

They went back inside to the front foyer. Her gaze traveled up the staircase to the second story where the bedrooms were. "Could we go upstairs and look around next?"

"Sure." He carried her luggage, shooing her away from helping him as they ascended to the next level. Once at the top, he pointed to the left and the master suite. He was assuming she'd sleep with him there, but would offer her one of his guest rooms, too.

The double doors leading to his master bedroom were

intricately carved in a design he loved. It wasn't like he'd spared no expense for this house or anything—with the exception of the premium security system he'd installed—but choosing a few personal touches had given him something worthwhile to do as he pondered the difficulties of his career path.

She opened the doors and said, "Ooh." Pleasure rushed through him that she liked her first look at his bedroom.

This was a first for him, too. He'd never brought a woman into his home before. At least not one he had a sexual relationship with. The idea of their tight bond happening so quickly registered. This same time yesterday, he hadn't known Chloe. Now he wondered how long they'd be together and admitted he wanted it to be a very long time.

While he didn't believe in one-night stands, typically his relationships were not long term by anyone's standards. It only took a month or so before the women he dated didn't care for his erratic schedule, of picking up and leaving for days on end with little or no contact until he returned from a job.

His last serious relationship had ended very badly because of his dangerous job. Shelley blamed him for what happened, but no more than he blamed himself. It was also the reason he hadn't dated anyone in well over a year. He was unwilling to participate in a string of meaningless one-night stands, but he also didn't want to endanger any more girlfriends due to his line of work. He hadn't wanted to put anyone he cared about in harm's way. Never again.

The idea that Chloe's intruder had been sent after him circled in his brain again. Why else would the guy have been dragging him out instead of pursuing Chloe?

"I love your bedroom," Chloe exclaimed, rushing forward into the large space. She went straight to his bed and seated herself on one side—his side—patting the surface in invitation.

"Afternoon delight?" he asked.

"I'd settle for a kiss."

"You should never settle."

Her eyebrows rose. "I'd hate to muss your sheets so early in the day."

"Meanwhile, that wouldn't bother me at all." He smiled, but wondered where his head was. Considering they were here because she needed protection, perhaps Deke should stop pursuing her, just like he should have done with his last girlfriend.

He and Shelley had only been together a couple of months. The majority of that time had been spent apart because his client had been chased after so relentlessly by the cartel. The guilty little secret he'd never told anyone was he'd planned to end it with Shelley before that job. He should have made a point of doing just that, but hadn't been able to see her in person before he left. Breaking up over the phone or especially with a text was very uncool, to his way of thinking.

Several weeks later, he'd finished that dangerous job, but it had followed him. Once the few remaining cartel members knew he had someone in his life, they'd gone after her as ruthlessly as they had him because they were vengeful bastards.

He and Shelley had been on their way to dinner in his car. Shelley hadn't known he planned to end it with her over dinner, of course, and then it had been too late to stop what happened. They rammed his car. It spun, flipped, and slid down a deserted stretch of highway. Stunned, Deke became aware he was upside down in his car, held in place by his seatbelt. He saw the hit man approach his vehicle, gun in hand, and wished he'd broken it off with Shelley before taking the job.

He shook off the disturbing memory, directing his

thoughts to Chloe. Was this a second chance to do things differently? Should he break it off with her now?

Deke tried to picture a huge breakup scene with Chloe at a big restaurant where he'd express his resolute lack of interest very publically so whoever might be after him could see clearly that he didn't care about her and that she wasn't going to be in his life anymore. Then again, he probably wasn't a good enough actor to pull that off. He never wanted to see Chloe's wounded expression if he told such a colossal lie.

No one would believe it anyway. Deke fairly pulsed with affection for Chloe every time he got within sensory range of her. Zak would call bullshit in a millisecond.

The object of his affection promptly kicked her shoes off and moved to the center of his bed on her knees, motioning for him to join her. He was weak. He wasn't ready to let her go. Would he ever be? Probably not. Therefore, he vowed to protect her until the issue of her safety was resolved.

Deke walked over to a panel on his wall hidden by a picture he liked. Instead of a safe behind the hinged door, he had an alternate security panel. He pushed all the necessary buttons to ensure his home's perimeter was secure and they were safe in his bachelor sanctuary.

Then he kicked his shoes off and joined her in the center of his bed.

She didn't waste any time on chat. She wrapped her arms around his neck and kissed him like she meant business.

Before he knew it they were rolling around on the comforter's surface, kissing wildly, shedding clothing and breathing hard. When they got down to underclothes, she worried about hurting his bruises from the night before, but he didn't. He pressed his hips between her bare open legs and flattened himself on top of her as their sizzling kiss continued.

Chloe twisted them until she was on top, straddling him. Breaking the kiss, she stared at where she'd bitten him and ran a thumb across his skin. "Are you sure that doesn't hurt?"

He grinned. "I'm positive." He'd never tell her that one of the thousand repeated questions at the hospital the night before had to do with whether the intruder had bitten him. She might never do it again.

Deke brushed his fingertip over the place he'd returned the favor, but he hadn't nipped her hard enough to leave a lasting mark.

Chloe bent to kiss his neck, nuzzling him with ferocious care as he wrestled with his libido, which urged him to simply throw her onto her back and take care of business.

She kissed his collarbone. She kissed the center of his chest. She kissed above his belly button. He wasn't stupid. She was headed to a very desirable place with her trail of kisses. Deke pushed out a long breath and let her do what she wanted. Her fingers slipped between the fabric of his briefs and his skin, drawing his only piece of clothing down his legs.

She dropped kisses slowly one after another along the length of his hard shaft. Letting her take her time was an exercise in restraint. He wanted her so much, wanted to feel her mouth on him in the worst way.

She gripped his cock in one soft hand, slid her lips around the very tip and sucked him into her mouth. His eyes rolled back in his head with the utter pleasure and intensity of her simple action. She moaned as she sucked him deeper into heated wet nirvana, the vibration of which put him at an even higher level of arousal.

Halfheartedly, Deke said, "Wait." He reached out, stroking his fingertips along the soft tendrils of her hair with the initial intention of pulling her away, as if to tell her she didn't have to do this, but he also didn't want her to stop.

His hand ended up on the back of her head, adding an extra resistance to her actions, making the experience all the better. She didn't seem to notice one way or another. In fact, she stepped up the intensity. One deep suck later and he lost control, groaning, arching, and tensing in the moment.

Deke heard bells ringing.

Were they in his head? No. They seemed familiar.

Chloe moved up onto her knees again and twisted her head over one shoulder. He was useless, flat on his back trying to remember his name.

"Is that your doorbell?" she asked.

The ringing sounded again. And again. And again. Just like at Chloe's place. Damn it. Had Ned found them?

With considerable effort, Deke sat up, hugged Chloe, kissed her cheek and said, "Unfortunately, yes."

He went to his security panel and brought up the front door camera feed. Zak was there with his forefinger lodged into the button. Deke flipped a switch, saying into the speaker, "Enough already. I'll be right down."

Zak gave him a surly raised eyebrow that said he better hurry.

Deke grabbed his jeans and pulled them on, noting that it seemed like he always had to get dressed in a hurry to answer a door of late.

"I'll be right back. Don't go anywhere."

"Who is it?"

"Zak."

"Oh. Should I come down too?"

Her moist, swollen lips were a dead giveaway as to what they'd just been doing. His brother didn't need any more ammunition. "No. I'll take care of it." He glanced at the cleavage straining against her bra. "You can be naked when I get back, if you want."

Her cheeks, as expected, pinked up nicely. "Okay," she said, a delicious smile of anticipation shaping her lovely features. He planned to reciprocate the attentions she'd so sweetly just given him.

Once he got rid of his brother.

He opened his front door briskly. Zak handed him the key to Chloe's house along with some paperwork and started to take a step into the foyer. Deke stopped him. "Not that I don't appreciate what you did, but I'm sort of busy."

His brother gave him a look that was difficult to interpret. At first he looked angry, but then his expression shifted to puzzlement. Zak's gaze went unerringly in the direction of his master bedroom. He didn't believe his brother was psychic, but then his face shifted to one of supreme amusement.

"What?" Deke wanted to get back to Chloe. Zak had likely just figured that out.

Zak pushed out an amused laugh. "Nothing. I'm just happy to see you with someone nice. I like her. Don't screw it up."

"I didn't screw it up the last time. That's what you told me, anyway."

He shrugged. "I know, but your ex wasn't right for you in the first place."

Deke frowned. Zak hadn't liked Shelley? That was new information. "Is that so?"

"Your ex wanted to be with a badass, and any badass would do. But she wasn't willing to stand by you when it counted." Zak pointed a finger in the direction of Deke's bedroom. "Chloe already cares for you. She was the very definition of frantic when we were on the way to the hospital last night. She blamed herself for what happened to you."

"I know. I'm not certain that's even true. It could well be someone from my past and not her idiot blind date."

Zak crossed his arms over his broad chest. "Not everything bad that happens is because of you or your job. Get over yourself already."

Deke huffed. "I know and I care for her, too."

"Good."

"Either way, I want to keep her safe, which is why I brought her here to my turf where I have it secured." His earlier notion of giving her up during a loud public breakup faded into the ridiculous. He dearly hoped it didn't come to that drastic measure.

"Also, the sex must be amazing, because don't think I didn't notice that bite mark on your shoulder." Zak winked.

Deke made a face, glancing over his shoulder toward where Chloe waited for him, naked. "Please don't ever say that out loud around her."

Zak grinned. "Okay, I won't *talk* about it, but you didn't notice the picture I snapped as they were loading you into the ambulance, did you? It's going straight into my *things to show our parents at the next Key West gathering* file."

Deke rolled his eyes, shut the door in Zak's face, reengaged the lock and alarm and headed back up to Chloe.

He opened the doors expecting to see her spread-eagle on his mussed bed. She wasn't in the room.

A moment of panic registered at seeing the empty bed until he heard a noise from the master bathroom. A smile shaped his lips as he recognized the sound of running water. He strolled in that direction, vowing to be happy with any place she'd chosen; shower, bathtub or even bathroom sink.

CHAPTER 10

After Deke left to answer the door, Chloe debated whether to wait and do a striptease once he returned or be fully nude upon his arrival. He'd not-so-subtly asked for her to be naked when he came back. Maybe she would save a striptease for later. She pulled her bra and panties off, depositing them on a chair.

She discovered it was very difficult to wait around in a strange room completely naked for an undetermined length of time. Where should her hands be? Draped above her head in repose as she stared into a corner? Resting casually on her thighs? Her belly? Her breasts?

He was taking longer than she expected. Then she noticed the door to the master bath. She scooted off the bed to see if it was as beautiful as the rest of his house. It was.

A wide hallway with four large closet doors lined up on either side led into an open space with a stunning oval bath—big enough for two people—centered in the main bathroom. Behind and above the huge tub was an intricately detailed stained glass window showcasing mostly black, white and gray glass with bits of red in a captivating asymmetrical pattern. The rest of the bathroom was black with white and gray marble.

The tile beneath her feet cooled her toes. She walked past the tub to check out the large etched-glass-encased shower stall. There were six showerheads and really two shower stations. No waiting.

The idea of a luxurious hot shower with more than one spray hitting her body was too enticing to resist. She turned the water on, noticing it steamed up and got hot quickly.

She put out a hand to test the water temperature just as Deke came into the room. "Are you showering? And if so, can I watch?"

"Yes. Or you can join me." She eyed a wide bench seat inside the stall and pictured all sorts of wicked things that could happen while she sprawled there.

"Need someone to scrub your back, do you?"

"Sure. In fact, I give you permission to scrub anywhere you'd like."

Chloe stepped under the spray, closed her eyes, and let the warm water ease over her head and down her body. Deke, warmly naked, was soon behind her. He dropped a kiss on her shoulder, wrapped his arms around her waist and simply held her. After a few moments he moved away.

When he returned, he had a soft bath sponge in hand. As promised, he soaped and scrubbed her back, her arms, her legs, and finally her front.

He softly moved the sponge over her belly, her breasts, and then below. She braced both hands on the shower walls as he touched her intimately, groaning with each sexy, deliberate stroke.

The slightly abrasive texture of the sponge sent spirals of pleasure through her each time he rubbed it across her nipples. When he pushed it between her legs, her knees almost buckled. Once he'd finished with the sponge, he shampooed her hair.

At first she was disappointed he'd moved away from

touching all her primary erogenous zones. Then his fingertips swirled in her hair, taking his time rubbing the soap into lather. She never realized having someone shampoo her hair could be such a sensuous exercise.

By the time he'd massaged every inch of her scalp and rinsed the suds away, she was ready to submit in any way he'd take her.

Standing behind her, Deke brushed a hand across her belly. She trapped it there with her hand. She also pushed her butt into his already stiff erection.

What if he stayed where he was and entered into her body from behind? A thrill ran down her spine at the very idea. She pressed her hips back then retreated a few times to hopefully express herself without speaking.

Deke moved away from her, but returned quickly after sheathing himself in a condom he'd brought along earlier. He kissed the back of her neck as he drew her out of the direct spray and placed her hands above her on the tile wall.

She eased her hips back, wanting him desperately. He obliged, as if reading her mind. His cock breached the slick entrance to her body. The angle was new and amazing and extra deep the moment he moved within her.

Once they were connected as intimately as possible, he not only moved inside her, he touched her everywhere, brushing her nipples with his fingertips until she cried out, on the very edge of losing it.

His thrusts were hypnotically arousing. When one of his hands slid between her legs to stroke her most sensitive place, she did lose it.

Enfolded in the now steamy confines of his luxury shower, Chloe's shrieks of pleasure echoed off the walls of this ethereal haven. He powered a few more deep, satisfying strokes into her body before he stiffened, grasping her body to his like he never wanted to let her go. He kissed the back of her neck before nipping her a few times along her shoulder. She shuddered in pleasure as his teeth caressed her skin with a bit more pressure than the last time.

Gentleman that he was, he rescrubbed her body, turned the shower off, toweled her dry, and then carried her boneless body back to his bed. They snuggled together beneath his soft sheets like they'd done it a thousand times before.

She dozed off thinking she'd be very happy here in his house, wondering how long she'd get to stay, knowing on some level any thought of leaving Deke was going to evoke a flood of tears the likes of which she'd never let loose before.

The sound of a loud, unfamiliar alarm woke her much later. It was evening, almost dark. She was pressed up against a solid heat source until Deke stumbled out of bed, taking his sexy, warm body away to go to the bedside security feed.

He pushed several buttons before the alarm finally stopped.

"What is it?" she asked, trying not to sound so panicked. "Is someone inside?"

"No. It was a perimeter breach of my property. But I don't see anything out there on the cameras."

"Could it be a dog or another animal?"

"It would have to be a big one. I have the weight sensors fixed so that animals don't usually set off the alarms. Maybe I need to change them."

He stepped away from the security panel and started getting dressed. "Wait up here. I'll do a quick check downstairs, but I'm sure it's fine. Don't worry."

While Deke was gone downstairs, Chloe found his T-shirt and put it on along with her panties. That was as dressed as she wanted to be. Her tummy rumbled, signaling they hadn't eaten since breakfast at noon.

"The coast is clear," he said when he returned. He also brought a tray of food. Either he'd read her mind or perhaps he heard her stomach growl from downstairs.

They ate sandwiches and sliced fruit on top of his rumpled sheets, feeding each other the last few morsels before the kissing started again.

"I see you found my T-shirt again."

"Yes. I hope you don't mind. I feel so sexy wearing it."

"I don't mind." He kissed her temple. "Let me take this back downstairs."

Deke left the room with the tray and was gone for longer than she thought he should be. Chloe tiptoed out of his bedroom to the bridge, looking on either side downstairs. There weren't any lights on, but ambient light from outside filtered in. Still, it was a bit spooky.

She inched forward another step, searching first the foyer and then the great room, expecting to see Deke searching or checking things. She saw nothing.

Chloe took three quick steps toward the staircase. She thought she saw a shadow out of the corner of her eye and shrieked like a banshee when the house alarm went off again. Her gaze went to the front door area and the other security panel she'd seen earlier.

Where was Deke? Did someone get him?

The first blare of the alarm was scary but not as much as when it stopped abruptly only seconds later. Had Deke turned it off or had someone else?

Deke stacked the few dishes in the sink and then did another full search of the lower level, including a trip out to his garage. He was checking each of the four stall doors there, ensuring the sensors hadn't been tampered with, when the perimeter alarm went off a second time.

Either there was a short in the wiring or someone was screwing with him. He'd suspect his brother, but knew Zak wouldn't toy with him after last night's intruder at Chloe's.

He had a small security panel installed in the garage and hit the button to turn the alarm off again as fast as he could. The noise was really annoying.

Chloe was upstairs, probably on the bridge, calling his name in an overloud whisper and sounding very worried.

"Chloe, I'll be right up."

"Deke?" She sounded very relieved. "Is it another animal outside?"

"Not sure." Maybe a two-legged animal trying to be cute.

He checked everywhere again and saw nothing. He felt like whatever had happened was intentional, but had no proof to show for it after another careful search.

If this was related to what happened yesterday, he'd have to more carefully think about who might be after him. Or trying to get to him through Chloe, like what had happened to his ex-girlfriend. And possibly the reason he should stay single.

Deke climbed the stairs to his bedroom. Chloe wasn't in bed. She looked like she'd been pacing.

"What's up?"

"Don't know."

"Should we be worried?"

He pushed out a breath. "I don't think so. It is a bit windy outside. It's possible something is hitting a sensor making it seem like someone is out there. Nothing has showed up on any of the cameras."

"How are you feeling?"

"Fine. Why?"

One slim shoulder lifted. "I'm supposed to be taking care of you. That's why we came here, right?"

"I thought we came here so *I* could protect *you* from idiot blind dates and intruder thugs."

"That, too."

"Are you tired?"

"A little."

"Want to get back in bed?"

"Yes."

They got back beneath his soft sheets and snuggled up again. They chatted about this and that, nothing and everything. Deke was lulled into a more secure feeling. The more he learned about her, the more he fell for her. She was perfect for him. He didn't know how long they talked—he'd deliberately stayed awake, expecting to hear the alarm—but eventually they dozed off in each other's arms.

Several hours later when the blare of his perimeter alarm sounded, Deke had his proof something was going on. Someone was out there playing with his security system, either trying to find a weak spot—good luck—or simply trying to catch him off guard. He'd seen this ploy before. Wear the owner down with repeated alarms until they become complacent, assume it's just a glitch in the system and either ignore further alarms or cut the system off altogether.

Deke planned to take every alarm seriously even if it went off a hundred times tonight. This time Chloe got up with him and clung to his back.

"I'm scared," she whispered as he scanned the security feed.

"I promise I won't let anything happen to you."

"What if they keep coming every few hours? What if they get inside?" Her hands slipped around his waist, her soft fingers digging into his abs. She was still wearing his T-shirt from earlier, which was sexy on so many levels he had to forcefully put his head back where it belonged.

"I have a safe room up here that we can use. No one can get us."

"Okay." She seemed to relax. She wasn't really very awake, which seemed to be part of the problem.

He scanned the perimeter again. The alarm set off this time was at the front door. He thought he saw the corner of a box on his stoop, but it was just out of his field of view. He didn't get worried until a check of the primary camera angle covering his porch showed nothing but black, as if someone had spray-painted it.

Deke backed up the recorded footage ten minutes and saw a man dressed completely in black with a ski mask in place throw a black bag over the camera. The man's type and build was very much like that of the intruder he'd tussled with at Chloe's. The guy was definitely wearing the same costume.

He wished he could see what was on his front porch.

He glanced at the clock, noting it was very early in the morning, still hours from dawn. Almost twenty-four hours ago, a similar-looking intruder had come in through Chloe's back kitchen door.

Deke had a bad feeling that this was not about her. It was about him and his job and his past and how he shouldn't be endangering someone else. The flash memory of brushing matted, blood-soaked strands of hair away from another feminine face gave him a jolt, the fear-inducing image keeping him focused on the task at hand. He couldn't let anything like that happen again.

Chloe's fingers pressed into him tighter, as if she could hear his wayward thoughts regarding what he'd say to break up with her spectacularly and publically enough that whatever bastard was after him would believe he didn't care about her. Did such painful words even exist?

Deke shut the security panel door and guided Chloe into the safe room. He'd had it installed after he bought the house, giving up a few square feet of closet space to accommodate it.

The room was hidden behind one of the racks of clothing in the master closet. The average person just looking wouldn't see any other space. But if you walked around the rack along the back wall and pushed the rack upward, the secret door opened.

There was a bed, food, water and a hard-wired phone line with a standalone Internet service that was completely separate from the one in the house.

Once he and Chloe were ensconced inside, Deke picked up the handset of the phone. He started to dial Zak's number, but hung up before he finished. Perhaps he'd call a different brother. One who could more easily deal with whatever was on his porch right now.

A sleepy Alex answered, "This better be good. I was having a really great dream that I'd like to get back to."

"It's Deke. I'm locked in my safe room. My perimeter alarm has gone off three times tonight in three different places. Any thoughts besides the obvious?"

Alex cleared his throat. "I don't know. Maybe it's a big neighbor dog wanting to frolic in your pool."

"Very funny. At first I thought it was a glitch, but it's possible someone is after me again."

"What did you do this time?"

Deke pondered the idea that he'd only kissed a stranger at a baseball game, thereby drawing attention to himself from any and all old enemies, foreign and domestic. However, he didn't want another brother razzing him about Chloe and the auspicious kiss cam incident, so he kept that tidbit to himself.

Besides, Zak would probably bring it up with their siblings at the first opportunity, so Deke didn't need to fan the flames or invite any more amusing brotherly antics.

"I'm not quite sure. It might be something from my

past. Or it might be a new threat." He laughed. "And come to think of it, that big Irish wolfhound down the street could be on the loose in my neighborhood, wanting to kick back and enjoy my awesome swimming pool."

"Considering that you so rarely need me for any reason, I'm on my way over."

"Wait. I saw through the security feed that someone dressed in black complete with a scary ski mask threw a bag over one of my security cameras and also left a package on my front doorstep that I can't see."

Chloe gasped at that detail. Deke threw her a reassuring look.

There was a pause on the other end of the phone line. "Way to bury the lead, bro."

"That's how I roll."

"Okay. I'll bring my gear along with me."

"Thanks, Alex. Oh, and one more thing."

"Now what?"

Alex was going to kick his ass, but his bodyguard mode wouldn't shut off and he wanted to ensure his brother didn't bring a legion of people with him tonight. Low profile was still his best option. "I know you're used to working with a crowd, but I wonder if you can limit the number of folks you bring along with you. I'd rather this wasn't official quite yet."

There was another long pause, long enough for Deke to consider that maybe a circus of law enforcement types might scare off the party responsible, which would be safer for Chloe.

Alex pushed out a long sigh as if he were truly tested by Deke's request. As a brother, Alex understood how Deke operated regarding his job. Low-key was always the best way to operate as a bodyguard. "Fine. I'll limit my crew, and make this a surprise practice field test. See you soon."

"Thanks, Alex. I owe you."

"Yes. You do. But you also know I'd do almost anything for my baby brother." Deke rolled his eyes, questioning his sanity at inviting yet another brother into his budding new acquaintance with Chloe.

Alex was his eldest brother. He liked lording it over the rest of the Langston siblings that he was superior because he was the firstborn and had claimed all the best genes. Alex was also fearless. He called himself a very successful bomb technician because he was still alive, but always said his prosperity was because he was cautious and methodical regarding the explosive aspects of his career. Pun intended.

Deke slipped the handset back onto its cradle and turned to Chloe. She'd been listening to every word. "Alex is another brother?"

He nodded.

Her eyebrows lifted. "I wonder if I'll end up meeting your entire family before the end of the night."

Deke shrugged, not at all worried about Chloe getting to know his family, just uncertain that he'd get to keep this relationship when all was said and done.

He motioned toward the bed in the corner. "Alex won't be here for a bit. Why don't we rest?"

She swallowed hard. "Someone left a package at the front door. Do you think it was the same guy?"

"Probably. He looked similar in build to the guy in your house."

"Do you think it's a bomb?"

"I can't say for certain, but that motive doesn't seem right to me. Whoever is doing this seems more like he's playing with us. A bomb would end the fun too soon. But we can't rule it out, so I called Alex, my bomb tech brother."

"I'm sorry I asked."

He laughed. "Don't worry. I mostly called him to

keep Zak from taking any more incriminating photos or video of us."

She only smiled momentarily, a stormy expression coming next. "I'm worried that whoever is out there has followed us to your house. I'm so sorry I brought this down on our heads. I'll bet you totally regret ever kissing me at that baseball game."

"You did not bring anything down on us." Deke pulled her into his arms and stared deeply into her mesmerizing green eyes, hoping she'd listen and believe him. "Besides, I have absolutely no regrets about anything I've done with you, publically or privately." He kissed the troubled pout from her mouth. "Don't worry. We'll figure this out." One way or another.

She didn't look convinced, but also didn't say anything else. She moved to the bed, curling up on top of the blanket instead of climbing between the sheets.

Deke followed her, snuggling behind her, dozing off for almost an hour before his phone rang. He looked at the display: Alex, likely calling to tell him he was ready to work.

"I brought the specialized equipment," his brother said, adding proudly, "and only three other guys."

"Great."

"I see the cardboard box centered on the porch. It's wide open at the top, but I can't see any contents from this distance. I'm sending the robot in. Remind me again about the specs on your safe room."

"Standard stuff. Fireproof, bulletproof and also hurricane proof up to two hundred-mile-per-hour wind gusts, although if Arizona ever has a hurricane in its path, we've got bigger problems than a box on my porch."

"Is your safe room bombproof, by any chance?"

"To a degree, sure. Depends on the payload. I don't

think we'd survive a nuclear blast at my front door, but maybe a lesser explosion."

"The robot is coming up to it. I see something. It looks square…like a… What the hell?"

"What?"

"The robot's camera is looking straight down into the box."

"Is it a bomb?"

"No. It's a framed picture."

"What?" Deke didn't expect that at all. "A picture of what?"

Alex grunted, but sounded amused. "You. It's a candid picture of you, bro."

"Alone?"

Alex laughed outright this time. "No. It's a kiss cam shot of you in a lip lock with some hot babe at a baseball game."

"No fucking way."

"Total fucking way. So who is she, Deke?"

CHAPTER 11

Chloe watched and listened to the call between Deke and his brother. They were talking about a picture.

"What is it?" she asked, unable to keep her curiosity at bay for a moment longer. "What's the picture of?" She expected any number of wickedly evil retribution type photos depicting malevolent things the man in the ski mask wanted them to fear he'd do once he caught up with them.

Deke looked at her, seemingly very reluctant to share. He finally said in a low, tight voice, "It's a picture of us at the baseball game."

Her mouth fell open in surprise. "The kiss cam shot?"

He nodded, then spoke into the phone again. "I'll be right down, Alex." Deke kissed her. "Stay here. I'll be right back."

"Wait. So there wasn't a bomb or any other threat?"

"No."

She followed him out of the room. He turned, stopping her as she plowed into his body. She slung her arms around his middle and hugged him tight. "Can't I please come down with you? I don't want to feel out of the loop in all of this."

He cleared his throat as if to impart bad news.

"Hopefully you won't take offense when I say that I'd prefer you not go downstairs in what you're currently wearing."

Chloe pulled away and looked down at herself, having forgotten she only wore his T-shirt and her skimpy panties. Maybe she'd developed exhibitionist tendencies after her recent induction into the *I love having sex with Deke* club. It always seemed like she needed to get dressed when she was with him. "Good point. I'll change and meet you down there."

He nodded, but looked like he'd much rather stuff her back into the safe room and lock it up tight than let her outside ever again. She went back to his bedroom, quickly slipped on the clothing she'd discarded earlier and hurried downstairs to keep from missing anything good.

Deke and another guy his size, dressed in what appeared to be riot gear, stood at the open front door looking down into a cardboard box.

"What is it?" she asked.

They both looked in her direction. Deke's brows furrowed and the other guy—his brother Alex, judging by the strong family resemblance—scrutinized her quickly and smiled.

In the reflection of the glass door, Chloe realized she should have probably checked herself in the mirror before prancing down here. She stuck her hands in her sex-tangled hair, finger-combing her locks, hoping the strand she'd just seen sticking up out of place was now tamed.

"Chloe," Deke said. "This is my brother Alex. Alex, this is Chloe."

"Ah. The hot babe in the picture."

"Nice to meet you, Alex." She stuck out her hand.

He grasped it in his gloved one. "Same here, Chloe."

She looked down into the box and saw a fancy, gilt-framed color photo of their first kiss blown up to an eight-by-ten landscape image. Even though it was scary how this picture had come to be here, her first thought was, *Great gift. I love it.*

A bright pink square sticky note fastened to the center of the frame at an angle bore the message, *Saw you at the game last night.*

It was sort of ominous, but there wasn't any direct threat to either of them. Perhaps the sender wanted to scare them with harmless gifts until they went crazy waiting for a more serious shoe to drop and for chaos to rain down around them. Meanwhile, the insidious sender would sit back and laugh, never intending to do more.

"Nice frame," she said. "Love the picture. I don't suppose I can keep it as a treasured souvenir?"

Alex said, "Sorry. I'm going to have to appropriate it to ensure there are no other unseen dangers, like poison spread on the frame or anything evil like that."

She nodded. "Good idea."

"Tell you what, though. If it isn't a weapon or poisonous, it's yours."

Deke said, "Are you sure there isn't anything underneath?"

"Gosh, I forgot to check. Let's do it now," Alex said with a mock horrified look on his face. He promptly rolled his eyes. "Yes. The robot arm lifted the frame up to check beneath. There is nothing else attached, like a bomb or device of any kind. We also X-rayed it and it's just a photo frame, a really nice one."

Someone dressed in riot gear similar to Alex's approached the three of them. He looked familiar. When he got close enough, she realized it was Zak.

"What are you doing here?" Deke asked.

"Alex called me. He said you didn't want a crowd. The better question is, why didn't *you* call me?"

Deke shrugged. "I figured I'd already abused your good nature enough for one day."

"Could never happen, bro," Zak said. He glanced at Chloe and nodded, adding a friendly, "Hey, Chloe."

"Hey, Zak."

He looked into the box and a grin surfaced. "They say a picture's worth a thousand words. This one is certainly getting lots of mileage."

Deke sighed. "Yeah, and I'm pretty tired of being harassed."

"No doubt."

"What happens next?" Chloe asked. "We aren't the newest candidates for witness protection, are we?"

Alex and Zak both smiled and looked at their brother.

Deke said, "Not quite yet. But we need to be wary and I'm not convinced staying here is a good idea at this point."

"Where can we go? My place is out."

Zak said, "I have a friend who might have a place you could use for a short while, but there are elaborate steps you'll have to take to ensure you aren't followed there, starting with the cover of darkness and evasive driving to ensure no one discovers where you're going." He turned eastward to the lightening sky. "I don't think we have time this morning."

Deke followed his stare toward the coming sunrise. "You're right. The sun will be up in a few minutes."

Twenty-four hours ago, she and Deke were leaving the hospital. She'd only known this man barely two days and now they were talking about safe houses and being on the run. She'd thought real estate was tough, but reconsidered in the wake of unwanted blind dates, intruders and now a crazy, trespassing masked guy leaving photo presents.

She was convinced she was to blame. They likely faced these dangers because of a horrible blind date set by her boss. She was already filing away some choice words for Justine the next time they spoke. If asked, would she deny giving a scary henchman her business card and then hiring him to harass them?

Chloe had a difficult time believing Justine could be so cold, even given her tone when they'd spoken last. She'd seemed desperate for her own business reasons to keep Ned happy. Maybe it truly was a coincidence the crumpled business card was in her house. Perhaps it had dropped from Chloe's purse long ago, falling out of sight until she happened to find it after Deke's brawl with the intruder.

Deke said, "We'll hunker down here until nightfall and then take you up on that safe house."

"Wait," Chloe said. "How long will we have to hide there? And what are we hiding from?"

The three brothers all shrugged in a totally identical way. One shoulder on each of them lifted and dropped quickly in unison as if they'd planned it in advance. She covered a smile.

"I only ask because eventually I'll need to get back to my job. I can't just leave it indefinitely. Are we being premature about a safe house?"

"I don't think so." Deke said, "Besides, I have some ideas for smoking out whoever is hunting us while we're safely tucked away."

"How long will it take?"

"Not sure, but I won't risk something happening to you."

"I still have to work. I mean, I could just hire you to be my armed bodyguard. We can drive around together while I open, show and sell houses. The truth is, I've always wanted a bodyguard."

The sultry look he gave her in that moment fairly singed her eyelashes. "We'll see." But just as quickly, he looked away, an uncomfortable expression coating his features. "Thing is, I don't typically date my clients."

"Well, then, forget I said anything." She was confident he could take care of her regardless of whether he shadowed her at her job. "If bodyguard is out of the question, then perhaps you could be my driver instead."

His frown deepened. Chloe wondered if she had somehow stepped over an invisible line with him, but wasn't certain how to get back on the right side of it to happy again. Her singular goal at this point was keeping Deke, regardless of any other matter. She didn't care if it was pathetic on her part or the stereotypical clingy girlfriend approach.

"Why don't you go on upstairs while we finish here, Chloe?" he said abruptly. "I'll be up in a little while."

And now he'd dismissed her. Not good.

Deke wasn't opposed to being Chloe's bodyguard in the literal sense, but the thought of being her driver made his mind go to memories he wanted to avoid, not repeat. The notion that he should simply enact a very public breakup to save her wouldn't go away.

Flashes of what had happened to Shelley saturated his mind even as he fought to shove them into the past where they belonged. The cartel was defunct. They couldn't have resurrected. No one was left to seek retribution. Right?

He hadn't been nearly as attached to his ex as he already was to Chloe.

She looked downright forlorn the moment he sent her upstairs. He wanted to take the words back, but his past relationship and the consequences of it kept him silent.

"If I'd dismissed my wife the way you just did Chloe, I'd be in the doghouse for a month. I'm surprised you didn't add, 'and don't worry your pretty little head about all these manly problems, babycakes' to seal the deal."

"Shut it, Zak."

"No. I won't shut it. You're going to lose her if you continue on this stupid macho path."

Deke leveled a look at Zak. "That would probably be for the best."

"What are you talking about, bro? What is in your head?"

The two men from Alex's team came to move the box into a safe container for transport elsewhere, keeping Deke's explanation at bay for a few minutes.

Once the three Langston brothers were alone on the porch again, Deke glanced over his shoulder to make sure Chloe wasn't on the stairs listening to their conversation. He pulled his front door closed for good measure, turned to them and said, "Remember my ex? Remember the accident and the guy who came after us back then? Do you also remember the shitstorm that transpired with the last woman in my life who was very unsafe because of my job when I ignored my gut?"

Zak gave him a surly look. "That was completely different and you know it."

"Regardless, I don't want a repeat. My feelings for Chloe are already stronger than they ever were for my ex. I need to protect her. I figure an epic public breakup should keep any and all crazies directed at me solely and most importantly off of her."

"Maybe not," Alex said. "The crazies already seem to know how you feel about Chloe. They went to a lot of trouble to send a picture and everything."

Zak shook his head. "Not only that, but what makes you think they're after you? Maybe it's her they want. Maybe you'll be leaving her open to the crazies you're trying to protect her from with a public dismissal like that."

"They came to my house."

"They started at her house first." Zak crossed his arms. "Maybe that intruder attacked you to get to her. Maybe he drugged you to get to her. Maybe he tried to drag you away in order to clear the field and get to her."

"Intruders and drugs?" Alex's eyes widened. "When did all this happen?"

Deke, ignored him and said, "They followed us to her house in my car not hers."

Zak rolled his eyes. "Are you with the psychic network now? You don't know that for certain. What if someone saw her kiss you at the game and flipped out?"

"Oh? Who would that be, the jealous kissing bandit? Someone who just happened to be at the game and saw us meet for the first time? Not likely. Our meeting was totally and completely random."

"All I'm saying is that she's in the picture, too. She's also here with you. You both came here together, right?"

"Yeah, in *my* car."

"So what? The last incident was at *her* house. They went to her house before ever coming here. I want you to allow for the possibility that whatever this is, it isn't because of you. Maybe someone has already been following her and the kiss sent them around the bend."

Alex tried again. "I'd like to hear the story of the incident at her house."

Deke ignored him again. "She's in real estate selling dream houses and making people happy, while I've been responsible for putting people in prison for bringing them down or keeping them from their heart's desire of killing those they feel are in the way." Deke shook his head. "So no. I doubt she's in danger because of her lifestyle. It can't be her. My gut is telling me that this is my problem and it's personal." His gut wasn't foolproof, and the bad feeling he had wasn't off the top of the scale, but still. This had to be on his shoulders not hers.

She'd be better off without him in her life causing

unintended mayhem. "They followed me there because we went in my car. Then we left her house in my car." Why didn't his brothers get it?

"Tell me this, hotshot." Zak cut to the heart of the matter. "Are you willing to bet her life on that gut feeling you're so proud of?"

He started to roll his eyes, but stopped and pondered his brother's question for a moment. Nothing was absolute. And the truth was, he *didn't* have a strong enough feeling about this. Just an itchy sensation in the back of his brain that things were off, aggravated by the guy breaking into Chloe's house and trying to drag him away, not her.

Then this picture frame incident the next night bolstered his resolve. It wasn't an outright threat. There was nothing actionable about some whacko nut job leaving a framed photo of the two of them with a vague note.

Plus, there had been ample time for the intruder to kill Chloe at her house before the police showed up if he was after her. But he hadn't, again making Deke feel like the target was painted on his back. Still, how could he be completely certain?

Alex, the voice of reason in their family, said, "I don't know exactly all of what's going on—since you won't tell me anything—but Zak is right, it's difficult to interpret what tonight's goal truly was about. Crazy yes, but the picture was of both of you and it wasn't addressed to either of you."

His brothers were giving him looks that said he should reconsider his gut feelings and allow for other possibilities.

"No. I guess I'm not willing to bet the farm on my gut feeling. At least not yet."

"Good answer," Zak said. "Do me a favor. Make a list of anyone from your past that you suspect might be capable of this. I'll use some of The Organization's resources to check them out. If everyone you suspect is jailed or otherwise unavailable due to death or dismemberment, you can maybe rest easy for longer than a couple of hours at a time. On the other hand, if I find anything significant then I'll talk to my handler and see about a safe house for you as a last resort and to give you further analysis time."

Deke nodded. "Thanks, Zak. I appreciate that and also both of you coming to the rescue, especially since this asshole only seems to harass us in the middle of the night."

Zak gave him a reassuring look. "No problem. Now go upstairs and make up with your girl. I suggest blatant groveling on your part."

Deke punched each of them in the shoulder and made a mental plan to do exactly that.

As they walked away from his porch, Alex asked Zak, "Will *you* tell me what happened at Chloe's house?"

"Sure," Zak said with a laugh. "I've even got some pictures to help clarify." Over his shoulder he winked at Deke, who managed to return a smile. His brothers were good guys, even when they were picking on him.

He didn't want to fight with Chloe and bore up to receive her anger, which he deserved. He approached his bedroom door with the idea she'd be super pissed and had every right to be. Groveling truly was his best option.

Chloe was pacing at the foot of his bed. When he stepped into the room, she turned and launched herself in his direction. His stomach fell to the floor when he noticed that she'd been crying.

He stiffened but caught her as she made contact, expecting her to start punching his chest with her fists and demanding the apology he owed her. Instead, she attached herself to him, buried her face into his throat and started crying again. She wrapped her legs around his hips.

"I'm so sorry," she whispered against his throat. "I know I'm to blame for all of this."

Deke needed to see her face and had to pry her off of him to do so. He set her on her feet. She pulled away, taking a long step back, but looked shrunken somehow, as if filled with severe regret. He inhaled deeply and exhaled to level his volatile emotions.

He'd done this. He'd made her feel this way. He was an ass.

Tears welled in her eyes again as she stood before him, not quite meeting his gaze as if fearful of what he'd say.

"I need you to look at me." She nodded slowly, a wary expression growing on her face, as if bracing for bad news. "And I also need for you to listen to me closely."

She tensed as if anticipating worse news. "I'm listening," she said softly, even as she stood a little taller.

"You don't have anything to be sorry for. I shouldn't have sent you away like I did. I wasn't thinking clearly."

"What?" Chloe's eyes narrowed in confusion. "But I'm the one who brought these problems down on us. I'd volunteer to leave, so you could be safe, but…" Her lips trembled. "It would break my heart."

"Doesn't matter," Deke said shaking his head. "I won't let you leave." He pulled her into his arms, hugging her tight. "And besides, you aren't to blame for this."

"How do you know?" Her question was muffled by his harsh embrace, making him want to squeeze her even tighter in apology.

"I don't know for certain who is after us, but I do

know that I need to say I'm sorry. I was a complete ass for sending you away like I did when we were downstairs. I'd like to beg for your forgiveness." He squeezed her harder and pressed a kiss to her cheek. "Also, I promise I won't do it again."

She sucked in a breath of surprise, leaning back to stare into his eyes, searching for he knew not what. Chloe moved forward until their lips were connected, and licked forcefully into his mouth. It felt like their first kiss at the stadium. She promptly wrapped her arms around his neck.

Deke hoisted her up and her legs moved to hug his body, one after another. Deke deepened the already volcanic kiss, rubbing his hands up and down her back.

He walked them over to the bed, bent down and pressed her to the mattress before pulling his mouth from hers. "I didn't mean to be so highhanded and dismiss you earlier."

"I forgive you. I know this situation is unique for both of us. No one would be at their best after what we've been through."

Deke stared into her face. "You're right. We've each been blaming ourselves for these rather extraordinary events. I believe we should consider a new tactic."

"Like what?"

"Maybe we should join forces and work together to keep our foes at bay."

A grin surfaced. "I like that idea so much better." She drew her fingertips down his face, the soft pads eliciting a prickle of sensation. He loved it when she touched him.

They kissed again. It was a softer kiss than the last few decadent ones. He liked that it went on for some time.

When his phone buzzed, he mentally cursed a blue streak at the interruption as he reached for his cell.

The text from Zak was a reminder to shoot him a list of contenders for the title of Midnight Perimeter Security Asshole.

Deke smiled and told him to keep his shirt on. And that he was busy and he'd send it later.

The final text from his brother read:

That means she forgave you already.
Like I said before.
You are one lucky son of a gun.

CHAPTER 12

It was late morning when Chloe startled awake in Deke's bed to the sound of her chirping cell phone. She sat up, noted she was alone again, and retrieved her phone from across the room where her clothing had ended up.

"Hello."

"It's Justine. Are you sure you can't make it to the open house today? Not even for a few minutes?"

Chloe would love to sneak away, if only to take the heat off of Deke for a couple of hours. Plus, if the house sold while Justine was there, Chloe's commission would be considerably less.

"Why? Has something come up?" She glanced across the room at the clock on the nightstand. The open house was scheduled to start in about two hours.

She walked to the bedroom doors and out into the hallway. She stepped to the end of the upstairs bridge across the house and looked down toward the kitchen, hoping to catch a glimpse of Deke. Was he cooking breakfast again? Or lunch?

She didn't hear anything. More specifically, she didn't smell anything good coming from the kitchen area. Where was he?

On the line, Justine said, "Not exactly. I just don't like working on the weekends."

Chloe swallowed the words of apology she was about to express and said, "It can't be helped."

"If I get a firm offer today that goes through to closing, it means the commission will be mine." Justine's tone had gone hard.

"I know, but I still get a percentage as the listing agent," Chloe said, worrying her bottom lip between her teeth. She hated giving over any extra part of her hard-earned income to Justine. Plus, she owed it to her clients to ensure their best interests were taken care of.

"Not as much. And there is something else for you to consider. Any new business created while I'm there would also be mine."

What the hell? "What new business? What are you talking about?"

"Mr. Henderson called the office looking for you earlier. He wanted to make sure you'd be at the open house. I told him I didn't think you'd make it. He sounded disappointed, but mentioned a new house search he wanted to discuss with you."

Chloe sighed, deeply upset she might miss out on an opportunity for Edgar Henderson's further real-estate business. The rich widower had been new to the area when he'd hired her last year to find him a house.

She'd spent an exhaustive amount of time locating the perfect home for him. He'd been so happy with her services and the final result, he'd given her a generous Christmas present. He'd also stopped by Premier Housing to visit her a few times, telling her he was about to be shopping for a second home as soon he sold a place he had in his former home town. That was probably what he'd told Justine about.

Chloe narrowed her eyes. "If Mr. Henderson stops

by, he may only want me to help him out with future ventures."

Justine huffed into the phone. "Well, I told him you were rather busy at the moment, taking some personal time. So naturally I offered to back you up. But if I do, then I get the full commission on any future business with him."

Chloe closed her eyes. Justine could be such a bitch. "I took one day of personal time, Justine, not a six-month sabbatical."

"I don't know when you'll be back, now do I? You haven't said."

"I'm taking care of a friend for a couple of days."

"You mean the stranger you took home from that baseball game, leaving poor Ned in the lurch?"

Wow. She really was in full-throttle bitch mode today. "Let's not get carried away. Ned went home with not one but two giggly young women from that same game. I hardly think he suffered."

"I believe you should call and talk to him, you know, make things right between the two of you."

She rolled her eyes. "No thanks. I've moved on. I encourage Ned to do the same. Feel free to tell him that for me."

"That would be a mistake." Hard-core bitch was still fully engaged.

"Not from where I sit. I suggest you let it go." Chloe wasn't ever speaking to Ned again. Not to say sorry. Not to make friends. Not to bail Justine out of whatever foolish promise she'd made him.

Justine was silent for several moments. Chloe figured wherever she was, she was pacing something fierce. Not getting her way regarding Ned had made her mad.

Chloe said, "Do you have anything else? I need to get going."

Justine piped up quickly and asked about several

completely unimportant office supply-related subjects before she hung up, obviously annoyed she couldn't get a rise out of Chloe.

Meanwhile, Chloe's mind chewed on the idea of showing up at the open house anyway. How could she make that happen? Her thoughts went first to Deke. He hadn't had any bouts of weakness or any symptoms that she'd seen since they'd left the hospital, although they'd mostly slept since they'd been here.

Should she go to the open house? Make nice with Justine?

The memory of the innocuous picture in the box when they'd been convinced it was a bomb or worse made her relax her attitude about any danger either of them might be in. The light of day always made everything less scary.

A noise to her left brought her out of her reverie. She turned and saw Deke enter the room fresh from the shower, his hair still damp, wearing only a towel slung around his hips. "You're up," he said. "I'd planned to let you sleep longer."

"Justine called."

"Your boss? Everything okay?"

"Yeah. I guess." Chloe shrugged and sighed deeply. "She's still giving me a really hard time about missing the open house today."

"When is it?"

"Not for a couple of hours yet, but it's at least a thirty-minute drive from here. Plus, I feel like I should get there early and help get things ready. Mostly I don't want to leave you alone after promising to look after you."

He shrugged. "If you want to go to this open house, I could go with you."

"Are you sure you feel up to it?"

"Yes." He grinned. "I'm perfectly fine." *Yes, you are.*

"Really? You'd do that for me?"

"Sure."

"Do you think it's safe?"

"As safe as anywhere. Do you have to let your boss know in advance? It's safer if no one expects you to be there. Could you just show up and take over?"

Chloe nodded. "Sure. Why not? We can take your car, and then I can keep an eye on you and also work."

"You just want to drive my sports car again."

She laughed, feeling so much better about this day than during her discussion with Justine. "Yes. You've found me out. I'm in lust with that sexy car of yours." *And I'm in love with you.* Chloe cleared her throat, trying to keep from shouting that volatile information out loud.

He hooked a thumb over one shoulder. "If you want, take a shower and get ready. I'll make us something quick to eat and we'll head out."

She moved closer, wanting to get at least a kiss and quick snuggle up with a towel-clad Deke.

Chloe laid her head on his damp shoulder, tracing a single finger down his chest, wanting to ignore the urge to work and instead spend another sex-filled afternoon with her new guy. "Thanks, Deke."

"No problem." He kissed her soundly and pushed her toward the bathroom or she might have changed her mind and lured him beneath the sheets instead.

An hour and a half later, dressed in her favorite navy suit, Chloe arrived at the open house early enough to put a few finishing touches in place. She was surprised Justine hadn't arrived yet to set up. She had learned some of her best open house tricks from the other woman.

She'd expected Justine to be in the middle of her

standard open house preparation and quietly cursing Chloe's name. Deke noticed right away. "I thought your boss was supposed to be here to work for you today."

"I thought so, too. Maybe she's running late because of traffic." Chloe didn't want to say it out loud, but had a bad feeling. Maybe Justine hadn't planned to show up at all. It would make her business look a little foolish, but the larger impact was on Chloe.

Deke put the *Open House* sign on top of the existing *For Sale* sign in the yard for her. Then they entered the home.

Chloe ticked off several prep items right away, finishing the moment a car pulled in the driveway a few minutes before the advertised start time. Was that Justine? She peeked out the living room window.

No. She saw two women get out of the vehicle, study the home's exterior and point to various features before moving to the front door for a tour. Chloe went to the front hallway to greet the first customers.

Where was Justine?

Deke stood next to her at the table where she'd placed the stack of brochures highlighting the list price and the home's unique features along with her business card stapled to the top of each sheet.

The two women spoke to her, but their full visual attention was on Deke and only Deke. Chloe found it hard to blame them. He looked amazing in a blue button-up shirt. His black jeans clung nicely to his fine ass, as she could attest, since she'd taken the opportunity to stare unapologetically when he'd put the *Open House* sign in place earlier.

"Are you the owner?" the taller of the women asked Deke.

Deke gave them what she considered a devastating smile and said, "No, ma'am. I'm with Chloe. I'm just helping out for the day."

The two turned to Chloe with envious expressions. "Well, we'll just take a look around then."

"Great," Chloe said exuberantly, trying to be understanding of these two ladies lusting after her guy. She handed each of them a brochure, pointing to the list price and features. "Let me know if you have any questions."

They nodded, each with another good look at Deke, before slowly sauntering off toward the master bedroom. Deke winked at her after they'd gone, but before she could say anything, someone else opened the door.

Five more couples with Realtors in tow showed up in the first half hour, and another three groups of interested buyers by the end of the first hour.

By the close of the second hour, yielding half a dozen more interested home shoppers, it was clear Justine wasn't planning to show. Chloe would have taken the brunt of any fallout from this fiasco had she not shown up.

She warred with herself about calling Justine to ask what the hell, but then Deke said, "Good thing you came here today. It looks like your boss is a no-show."

"You're right." Chloe's anger had steadily increased as more and more time went by. She'd never asked Justine to cover for her in the four years she'd worked at Premier Housing. She reached for her phone, then stopped. She was too angry to discuss anything with Justine right now. She'd end up leaving Premier Housing before she was ready to go out on her own. She wasn't going to let Justine rile her up right now.

"Do you think this is payback for what happened with the dickwad date she set you up with?"

She nodded. "Probably. But it's so unprofessional."

"Maybe she got held up at another house or something."

Chloe shrugged. If that was true, wouldn't Justine have called to let her know?

Another thought made her ashamed of herself. What if Justine was in trouble? What if she'd had an accident?

Chloe went from anger to concern in a heartbeat. She dug her phone out of her purse and called Justine's number as her stomach dropped to the floor.

Before Chloe could even offer a simple greeting, Justine said, "I'm very busy with your open house right now, Chloe. What do you want?"

What the hell?

The short-lived worry she'd felt went straight back to fury. Justine was lying. Chloe recovered quickly, answering, "I wondered how the open house was going. I guess it's going well if you're so busy. Want me to call back later?"

Out of the corner of her eye she saw Deke's brows go straight up in question, then a second later a light smile played on his beautiful mouth.

There was a long pause on the phone line. "No. This open house isn't really going that well, Chloe. Honestly, except for the neighbor currently wandering through the place, there hasn't been much going on here."

"Is that so? That's interesting. I expected a pretty busy day."

"Seriously, did you even advertise this open house?" Justine asked. "I mean, it's kind of a dud. None of the people who showed up today are much more than neighborhood looky-loos, checking out the house for sale on their block to see what their own property is worth."

It was quite a shock to discover what an incredible liar Justine was. If Chloe hadn't been standing in the center of the open house with a witness, she might easily have believed Justine and her fable about the open house being ineffective when the other woman hadn't even shown up at all.

In the background noise through the line wherever Justine really was, Chloe distinctly heard someone talking on another phone. She closed her eyes to concentrate on why the voice sounded so familiar. She kind of expected it to be Ned's voice, with Justine spinning him some false yarn about how Chloe was so sorry for what she'd done and couldn't wait to make up with him.

But then the voice said good-bye over the phone using an odd, old-fashioned sentiment and she knew exactly who Justine was in the same room with. *What the hell?*

Her face went flame hot. It was her client, Mr. Henderson, the rich widower who might stop by the open house, which was the singular reason Chloe had made an extra effort to be here.

"I did advertise this place, heavily."

"That was a waste of money."

"No it wasn't."

"How do you figure?"

Chloe inhaled a deep breath, ready to end the charade. "I'm here right now at the open house where you aren't. I've already received a trio of very interested offers. One of which is for cash."

"What? You're at the open house right now?" Justine asked as if shocked her little ploy had been revealed. "I thought you said you had to take care of someone."

"Since I just heard Mr. Henderson's voice where you are, I'm certain you did this on purpose. Are you at the office? Did you lure him there to steal his business from me or does he think I'm going to show up there and you've made me look bad and miss him?"

"I don't know what you're talking about."

In the background, Chloe heard Mr. Henderson say,

"Where is Chloe? It isn't like her to be late for a meeting."

"Gotta go." Justine hung up.

Chloe lowered her arm, counting slowly to five in order to keep from slamming her phone onto the lovely travertine tile entryway where she stood.

If she hadn't needed to stay at the open house for another hour she would have high-tailed it over to the office, hoping to catch Mr. Henderson before he left or signed a new ironclad contract with Justine. Not to mention there were people still in the house.

Chloe would have called Mr. Henderson to let him know where she was, but while the man carried a cell phone to make calls, he didn't typically accept calls on it.

He'd told her repeatedly that he preferred to only talk on his landline at home when receiving calls. Not to mention the fact that anyone calling his home phone couldn't leave a message. He didn't like gadgets or technology. He was a little bit old-fashioned all the way around, but he'd been very generous to her bottom line, ranking easily as her very best client. But maybe not for long.

"What's up?" Deke asked. She jumped, so angry she'd forgotten not only where she was but who was with her.

"I just discovered Justine is more hard-core bitch, thief and liar than I realized."

"Oh, yeah? So she never planned to be here?"

"No. She didn't. She likely engineered this whole thing to steal a client of mine." Chloe's mind spun with all manner of suspicions as this new information circulated.

Would it be so farfetched to believe that Justine had set up this whole intruder-slash-invader rigmarole to keep Chloe away from her clients? Or rather one very lucrative client in particular?

"That's messed up," Deke said.

Chloe turned to him. "I wonder if Justine is behind all our intruder issues."

"What do you mean?"

Chloe told him what she suspected was going on with Mr. Henderson in Justine's office at this very moment. "I've likely lost my best client. What do you want to bet me that after today, we won't have a single problem with anything regarding intruders or perimeter breaches? She's going to sign him to an exclusive contract, and then our worries will be at an end."

Deke shook his head. "Doesn't mean I'm going to lower my guard."

"That's okay. I wouldn't expect you to."

She pursed her lips and crossed her arms. Her gaze was focused on nothing as she contemplated the last several days. "At one time I never would have believed Justine could be capable of something like this. She's always been ruthless, but this seems crazy. Now... I don't know. She's been acting so erratically lately that maybe she is capable of this. I believe it. Now that she has what she wants, I expect we won't have a single bit of trouble going forward."

"If it's true, I'm sorry you lost your best client."

Chloe shrugged. "Maybe I haven't lost Mr. Henderson. Maybe he won't like Justine. Maybe he'll stick with me."

"He'd be a fool not to. So do I need to be jealous of this rich client?"

"Jealous? Of Mr. Henderson?" Chloe laughed. The tall yet slightly stooped, snow-haired old gentleman with the dapper attire and last century's attitudes was no threat to Deke at a romantic level. "No. You truly don't."

Deke wrapped an arm around her shoulder, kissing her anger away with a single lick.

The front door opening suddenly pulled them apart, but the couple coming inside to view the house had obviously seen them kissing. They smiled, accepted a brochure, and moved toward the kitchen.

By the time the open house was over, Chloe had mixed emotions regarding the future of her career. On the one hand she was grateful she and Deke weren't in any true danger. She was convinced Justine was behind their intruder problems.

On the other hand, this episode proved to her it was time to leave Justine's brokerage and go off on her own. But she refused to allow Justine to push her out. She'd accelerate the plans she already had in place, but most importantly, she'd leave Premier Housing on her own terms when she was good and damn ready.

CHAPTER 13

Once the open house had ended—a half hour late because of enthusiastic people unwilling to leave until they'd gotten Chloe's personal attention—Deke slung an arm around her shoulders and hugged her. "Impressive," he said with a healthy amount of admiration in his tone.

"What was?"

"You are." He kissed her firmly on the lips for the first time without having to worry about being caught by prospective homebuyers. He'd never kissed a client before, during or after a security assignment either.

She shrugged. "What did I do that was so impressive?"

"You didn't punch anyone in the face for asking the same damn question over and over again even though all the information they asked about repeatedly was clearly in the brochure you provided."

She laughed. "Punching people in the face is more up your alley, I think."

"That could very well be true. Okay, so now what?"

"Now I have to go into the lion's den or rather Premier Housing to process these offers and hope Justine isn't there. I don't know if I can trust myself in her presence right now."

"That means I definitely need to go with you for protection."

"Mine or hers?"

"I'd say both, but I only care about what happens to you."

"You know what? If you take me back to your place, I can file them using my laptop."

"I'm happy to do that, but you'll have to face her eventually."

She looked skyward as if debating two very difficult decisions. "You're right. I'm not going to let her dictate my professional life. If it were any other day, I'd go immediately to the office and get the ball rolling. Since you'll be there, I have no excuse not to. I need to let the owners know the status of their property and the results of this very successful open house."

Luckily, Justine was gone for the day by the time they reached Premier Housing. They also didn't see Mr. Henderson loitering around anywhere outside, although Chloe looked for him on the way inside. Deke parked himself in her office chair and watched her work.

Deke wasn't ready to let go of his private assertion over who was responsible for both of the intruders at their homes, but he was willing to allow for the possibility everything could have been orchestrated by her boss.

He hoped Chloe was right, because she was amazing and he didn't think he'd be able to end things with her. Especially not in any sort of public display, lying through his teeth about how she didn't mean enough to him and that he could never really love her the way she deserved. *Wasn't that the speech I practiced to tell Shelley?* While the substance of his message had been true of his ex, it was not the truth regarding his feelings for a very exuberant real estate agent who lit his heart up with her mere presence.

He could definitely love Chloe. Maybe he already did.

Deke was beginning to believe Chloe had been right. Two weeks had passed, and nothing untoward had happened at their homes or anywhere else in their presence.

Maybe Justine Keller-Howe really was behind everything.

Alex had done a thorough check of the framed photo left on his doorstep. There hadn't been any poison that could permeate the skin, killing by touch. He'd found only a small wireless voice transmitter and listening device embedded in the frame as part of the design. It had unlimited distance and could be accessed by pretty much anything, including a cell phone.

Someone had wanted to bug Deke's house? Had they foolishly thought he'd see the picture of him kissing Chloe and promptly bring it inside to display like it was a gift from a secret admirer with good intentions?

Talk about too stupid to live. Alex promised to debug it and send the framed picture back to Chloe, as requested.

Meanwhile, the substantial list of names he'd given Zak to check with The Organization's resources had all come back negative for activity in the area. Only two had been in a position to accomplish any breaking and entering or trespassing mischief, but neither of them had the ready resources to achieve what had been done. Private mercenaries tasked with mayhem and tranquilizer shots weren't cheap.

He'd even made Zak check for any hint of new or

recent cartel involvement and that was also a complete bust.

Even so, Chloe had gone about her business with him shadowing her like a hawk at each home showing and open house like he would bite any hand that even waved in her direction. He didn't leave her side regardless of what she was doing.

The first week she'd given him that *I told you so* look each and every day. By the second week, he was giving it to himself in the mirror. Currently, they couldn't buy anyone's attention.

Not that they went out of their way to get any, but there had been no more break-ins at either of their homes. No one seemed to be following them. None of Chloe's clients gave off any bad vibes. Through it all, Deke did his best to keep her safe like he would a paying client, yet give her the space she needed to do her thing.

No one made a move or hinted at wanting to make a move beyond trying to buy whatever home she was selling. She'd sold four in the past two weeks. He didn't know if that was good or not. Was he cramping her style?

"I'm not scaring off your clientele, am I?" he asked as they drove up to another house showing and parked in the driveway.

"Not even close. Having a super sexy bodyguard hovering around has increased my sales substantially. I think that's because all of the women think you come with whatever house we're showing."

He shook his head. "I doubt that very much."

"I don't. You're hot."

"I'm glad you think so. Yours is the only opinion I care about, though." They kissed passionately for several seconds. Deke broke away when another car pulled into the driveway where they'd parked to wait.

She quickly showed the home and the clients seemed very happy, promising to call her soon with a decision about whether to put in an official offer.

On the way back to his house, they stopped at her place long enough for her to pick up a few more items for her continued stay at his place. They also stopped to grab a bite of lunch.

Technically, they were living together. It wasn't something that had been formally discussed, but they'd found a nice rhythm of day-to-day living that he enjoyed very much. Deke was delighted she was here in his home. He certainly didn't mind waking up to her each and every morning. In fact, over the last couple of weeks, she'd moved a substantial volume of clothing and personal things to his home and master bedroom. He'd given her half the space in his closet, telling her she could have more if she needed it. Even with his regular clothing and his tactical gear, he used less than a fourth of the available space in his closet.

Having Chloe here every day practically since they'd met had been as seamless as if they'd always been together. He liked it better than living alone and once this matter of her safety had been resolved, he hoped she'd just remain with him.

It was early afternoon by the time they got back to his place. The moment they set foot inside, his phone rang in his pocket. A check of the screen revealed it wasn't one of his brothers or his parents. Chloe went upstairs to put her things away as he fielded the call.

The person at the end of the very poor connection said he was a friend of someone Deke had worked with several years ago. Deke hadn't been in touch with that friend for about the same length of time, but appreciated the career connection after all this time.

He'd been avoiding doing even short-term security jobs in favor of following Chloe around. Not that he minded, but perhaps it was time to get back on the horse, so to speak.

"I'd like to talk to you about a security job." There was a lot of noise coming through the line, making it sound like the guy was calling from Mars or something.

"What kind of security job?"

"I'd really rather explain it in person," the man said through the static.

"When do you want to meet?"

"Now, if you're available." Deke was about to say no, he was busy, but sent his gaze to the second floor briefly. Chloe was finished for the day. He hadn't so much as fielded a call for his own business since the baseball game where he met Chloe.

"I understand that it's short notice," the man said sincerely. "The thing is, I have a location I'm considering for some events coming up. I'd like your opinion on how much security it would take for the space. What could be covered with surveillance and what would I need for security guard coverage."

This was actually Deke's favorite type of job. He could go in, assess the structure and give fairly accurate numbers regarding the best security for the most reasonable price and be done in less than a day.

"How big is the place?"

"About ten thousand square feet total on two floors." In other words, a cakewalk. The guy then recited the address, which was fairly close, only about twenty minutes away.

If Deke could get Chloe to stay in his house for the afternoon, he'd do it. "I should be able to meet you in half an hour, but let me check on something and I'll call you right back."

"Fair enough."

Deke climbed the stairs two at a time. Chloe was in the master bedroom closet, hanging up three more business suits. He leaned a shoulder against the open doorway and watched her.

He'd never lived with anyone before, but spending the past two weeks with Chloe had been amazing. They slept together each night in his large bed, whether or not they made love. They ate their meals together, sharing the cooking and cleaning up like they'd done it together for years. She was easy to be with and he liked talking to her. He'd even enticed her into the hot tub a few times to relax. It had become an end of the day practice he looked forward to each and every night, especially now that he had someone to share it with and talk about life.

After two weeks of perfect bliss, Deke wondered if they'd just remain together from now on. The idea of moving her things out was distasteful. He quickly shoved that prospect to the far back of his mind.

"Hey," he said quietly, knowing she'd jump regardless of his volume.

As expected, she startled, and turned around, nearly dropping a cream blouse onto the floor. But still she grinned at him. "You scared me."

Deke needed to tell her he was leaving, and ask her to remain locked in his secure home. But first he wanted to touch her and kiss her and…well, anything else would take too long, but his desire for her wasn't easy to put on a shelf.

"I just got a call from a new client wanting me to assess the security on a property. I'll go, but only if you promise to stay here nice and safe within the security perimeter of my house."

"Okay. I'll stay. Nice and safe right here." Chloe tilted her head to one side. "Or do you want me to go with you? I could take notes or something. And it's only fair, since you've been shadowing me for weeks now."

He shook his head. It would take him too long to assess the property and watch over her at the same time.

"Nice of you to offer, but I can get done faster if you aren't there to distract me."

One eyebrow rose gently. "Oh? I distract you, do I?"

"Every single day." She smiled, hung her blouse on the rack and approached him.

"I need you to promise me that you'll stay in the house," he repeated, trying not to sound like, well, a hard-assed bodyguard dictating her life.

She shrugged. "I'm not planning anything else today."

"But if some stranger calls to look at a house after I'm gone, please schedule it for when I can go with you."

She sighed. "I honestly believe it was Justine."

"But she hasn't admitted it."

"Of course not. She's as pure as a fresh snowdrift, and it's been weeks now."

"Only two weeks."

She shrugged. "I don't expect anything to change."

"I won't let my guard down, Chloe. Promise me you won't leave the house to rush off and show any houses to strangers without me to watch over you."

She looked skyward as if for strength, but he could tell she was teasing him. "Okay. I promise. No showing houses to strangers. Do we need to perform a blood oath or anything before you go?"

"No. I trust you."

He kissed her softly, meaning it to be quick, but that didn't work as he'd anticipated. Moments later, she'd pinned him to an open wall, wrapped both arms around his neck, and started rubbing her body against his in invitation.

"Do I need to satisfy you before I go?"

She pushed out a mock long-suffering sigh. "No. You can go and do your job. It's only fair. I'll be here when you get back, waiting in bed. Or perhaps I'll cook." Her head tilted to one side as if she pondered the pros and cons of cooking for him or waiting in the bedroom for him. Either one worked, because they could eat and then go to bed or reverse it. And now he had something to look forward to when he got back.

"Perfect." He kissed her once more, called the potential client to confirm he'd be there in thirty minutes—giving himself an extra ten minute traffic allowance—and left in his SUV after securing her inside his home.

Deke made great time, arriving at the location ten minutes early. He'd taken a shortcut on some questionably maintained back roads leading to the fairly bleak industrial area.

He got out of his vehicle, assessing the property for what kind of security would be needed. The place looked bigger than ten thousand square feet, but maybe the guy had estimated wrong.

Deke walked the perimeter of the building, noting the number of exits from each floor, and making a mental list of requirements for whatever level of security this potential client had in mind. Often price determined how secure a place would ultimately be.

One corner of the building looked like it was pushed into a hill, but when he rounded the corner he saw a loading dock. It looked like there might be a basement as well.

The guy had said two stories, not three, although some people didn't count a basement in the total square footage or for security purposes if they didn't plan on using it. It would have to be addressed in his proposal, though. Deke would have to see if there was a full lower floor once he got inside.

Rounding the corner to the front of the building where his vehicle was parked, he pulled his phone out to check the time, and noted the client was already over ten minutes late. For some reason, he'd gotten the impression the guy was waiting here for him, which was why he wanted Deke here so fast.

Deke thumb-dialed the most recent contact, but it didn't go through. He tried again to no avail, and realized he had no service. He walked closer to his vehicle, which had a built-in hot spot, but his phone did not find any signal at all. Very odd. What was going on?

He spun around, looking at everything and nothing, seeing no threats, but knowing something was seriously wrong. He moved closer to his vehicle, trying to get phone service.

The one and only time he hadn't been able to get a signal using his hot spot was when a friend was testing the range of a signal jammer.

Deke stopped. His body went rigid at the idea now dancing in his head.

Was there a signal jammer somewhere nearby? He turned to look at the building again, seeing nothing to indicate it was being readied for any use at all.

The gut feeling he'd been ignoring since leaving Chloe alone at home ripped open a hole in his belly. He fairly leapt back into his vehicle, started it up and headed home, taking his shortcut at a dangerous speed.

He kept trying to dial out but the signal remained blocked. He was half a mile from the building before he got a single bar of service again. If a jammer was in play back there, it had been a very big and expensive one.

His first call was thumb-dialed to Chloe's cell. She didn't answer. He tried again. Nothing. He left a message, which he barked into the receiver. "Chloe, do not leave my house! Call me the second you get this message!"

The only time she didn't answer her phone was when she was driving. She didn't even use hands-free stuff. *Fuck.* He should never have left her. What had he been thinking? He'd let his guard down a mere fraction and chaos reigned again. *Fuck.*

Memories of his ex being carted off in an ambulance because of the last time he'd ignored a gut feeling flooded his system with self-loathing and regret. He pushed the gas pedal down harder, inching his speed higher. Luckily for everyone on the road today, there was little traffic on his way home.

Phone pressed to his ear, continuing to dial Chloe's number repeatedly, Deke heard a beeping sound signaling a new phone message coming through. He squealed into his driveway, shoved the shifter into park and pushed the buttons to listen to the message as he exited his vehicle and ran for the front door. The time stamp said the message had been sent when his phone was jammed at the bogus security job location about twenty-five minutes ago.

Chloe's voice came through. Relief flooded him just hearing her voice, until the gist of her message resonated. "Deke, I'm on my way to show a client a house. Don't worry. It's only ten minutes from here and it's someone I know very well. In fact, it's Mr. Henderson. No stranger, I promise. I'll likely beat you back to the house, but in case you get done early and want to be my bodyguard, here's the address. I want to ensure you aren't jealous." With amusement in her tone, she recited a street and house number, which was indeed close by.

Deke jumped back into his SUV and had the shifter slammed into reverse before the rest of her message was completed. He was racing into traffic seconds later. Jealousy was not the issue. Chloe's safety was.

He tried to call her cell again. It went straight to voicemail. Dread coated his insides. Deke could feel utter dismay trying to smother him. The amount of acid splashing in his belly could dissolve the entire surface of a planet. This was so bad. This was so very, very bad.

CHAPTER 14

Chloe finished hanging up her clothing as Deke left the house. She heard the garage door close and only a few minutes later she got the call from the client she assumed she'd lost. Mr. Henderson.

She recognized his number and answered with a vibrant, "Hello?" Inside she bounced up and down with eager relief. Perhaps her best client wasn't lost to Justine after all.

"Greetings, Chloe," Mr. Henderson said. "Have I called you at a busy time?"

"No. Not at all, Mr. Henderson." She tried to still her racing heartbeat. Maybe he *hadn't* signed with Justine. "What can I do for you?"

"As you know, I've been looking for another home in the area."

"Yes. Of course." Chloe would not even mention Justine's name. Hopefully, he hadn't signed anything exclusive with her scheming boss. "How can I help you?"

"A friend of mine sent me a home listing from the local newspaper that looks very promising indeed." Chloe smiled. Mr. Henderson was not a fan of technology. He still lived in the world of newspapers and business trips out of town. "I know it isn't terribly far away from my current home, but it looks like a real peach. I'd love to see it, if you're available to show it to me. I wanted to get a quick look today before I leave on a business trip later this afternoon."

Chloe had promised Deke she wouldn't show any houses to strangers. But Mr. Henderson was a well-known client. Her best. At least she hoped he was still her client. "What's the address, Mr. Henderson?"

He recited it to her slowly and carefully. She wrote it down on a pad on the nightstand. It was only five, no more than ten, minutes away from Deke's house depending on traffic.

"I know this is very short notice, but is there any way we could meet there in twenty minutes or so? I'd really like to get a look at this place. I don't want to lose out because of my trip."

Chloe closed her eyes for a moment, pondering her options. As angry as she was at Justine for trying to steal a rich client, she wouldn't do the same thing. It wasn't her style. "Can I ask you a candid question, Mr. Henderson?"

"Certainly."

"Did you meet with my broker, Justine, a couple of weeks ago?"

"Well," he said slowly. "I called the office asking for you. Justine told me you were taking care of a sick friend, but that you might be able to meet at the office. When I got there, she said you couldn't make it, but that she wanted me to sign a paper so she could be my sole representative."

Chloe closed her eyes and pushed out a resigned breath.

Mr. Henderson continued, "But I didn't want to do that before speaking to you, Chloe. So I didn't sign her paper. Then I left for a business trip later that same day.

And I only returned this morning. I'd forgotten all about it, to be honest. Is there a problem?"

Chloe did a silent joyful dance of victory. So, Justine had failed. "No. I wanted to make sure you wanted me to remain your agent and not Justine. If you'd signed that paper for her, I wouldn't be able to represent you without consulting with her first."

There was a pause at the end of the line. "No. That wouldn't do at all. I feel like we do very well together, Chloe. I'd prefer to keep *you* as my personal representative from now on. Will that be all right?"

Chloe practically sighed in relief at this excellent information. "Yes. It will. Thank you, Mr. Henderson. I believe we work well together, too. I'll meet you at the address in less than fifteen minutes."

"Until then, I'll bid you good day," Mr. Henderson expressed his typical old-fashioned goodbye. She found it endearing.

Chloe sent a text to the listing agent, asking to see the house as soon as possible. She used her phone to look up the specs on the place he wanted to see.

A minute or two later she received a return text that the home was ready to show along with the specific information she'd need to get inside.

She quickly put on one of the suits she'd just hung up, went down to the first stall of the four-car garage where Deke had given her space for her vehicle. She exited through the laundry room, pushing the button for the garage door to rise. She closed the door firmly, reset the alarm and pulled her car out. Before she left, Chloe called Deke to let him know where she'd be even though she would probably be back well before he returned.

Chloe made good time to the address. It was a high-end property—one of the most expensive listings in town—with lots of land, a very long driveway leading through an arched portico and onto a very large paver stone parking area at the rear of the house. There was a spacious four-door oversized garage at one end of the huge U-shaped home and another three-door oversized garage at the other end.

After ten minutes, she got out of her car at the back of the house and went to ensure the entrance code for the lock box would work. The device cover opened easily to reveal a key, which she used and put back, placing a wedge she always carried at the base of the door. She stepped inside a spotless, palatial kitchen that likely cost more than her entire house and maybe even more than Deke's place. She dropped her purse, keys and file folder at the end of the counter by the door.

The centerpiece that drew the eye in the impressive kitchen was a huge hammered-copper stove hood stretching all the way to the top of the twelve-foot ceiling. Black and gray granite countertops lined three walls in a complimentary color and covered the massive island centered in the room.

A glance at the security panel revealed the alarm wasn't set. Had it been turned off to accommodate showings? Chloe made a note to recommend to the selling agent that the owners keep the security in place. Like Deke said, there was no sense in having locks and security if you weren't going to use them.

Chloe crossed the room between one side of the island and the stove and headed to the sizable butler's pantry, making her way to the inside access to the four-car garage. Perhaps she'd open a couple of the doors so when Mr. Henderson got here he could see the space.

Mr. Henderson had several classic cars and a couple of other antique vehicles. The first thing he always wanted to look at was the garage space. He'd love that the seven stalls advertised in this listing were huge.

She also couldn't help calculating her approximate commission should a deal go through at the price listed.

It would certainly be a bountiful year, but she tried not to make that her focus. Helping Mr. Henderson find the perfect place was where she needed to center all her efforts. That was what made her successful, not worrying about grasping every penny she could at the expense of her clients' happiness.

Chloe's goal was to always ensure her clients were ecstatic with the choice they made in a home purchase. She was bright and happy and excited about each and every home she showed anyone she represented, hoping each listing she presented would be perfect for them. And even if it wasn't, she took pride in listening to what her clients did or didn't like and incorporating those comments into the next house showing.

Occasionally, clients chose their perfect place after only seeing three to five houses, but usually it took many more. Her record was forty-seven showings in four weeks before getting a grandmotherly type to finally choose one. It never surprised any Realtor in the business that the elderly woman ended up purchasing the first house she looked at.

Mr. Henderson had also put her through her paces with about thirty showings in just over two weeks. Her commission was worth it for Mr. Henderson and not as much with the grandmotherly type. But such was life in this business. She tried to take it all in stride, convinced that everything balanced out eventually.

Chloe unlocked and opened the door to the garage, stepping down into a vast gloomy space. Light filtered in through the very tiny, decorative windows in the garage doors. The closest stall had a large silver SUV parked in it, which was a bit unexpected. The house information she'd quickly scanned said the place had been vacated for sale. Maybe the owners hadn't moved the vehicle yet or had forgotten about it.

Her life wasn't such that she could forget such a large

possession, but this wasn't the first time it had happened.

Chloe took three more careful steps down into the garage space, reaching to her right, fingertips searching along the wall to find the light switch.

She flipped the first switch she came to and nothing happened. She tried the second and the third ones along the row, and still nothing. Oh no. She hoped the power was on. Usually even if no one was currently living in a house, the owners left the electricity and water on for showings, especially when it involved a house in this lofty price range. Then again, the security was off, too. Maybe the owners thought they were saving lots of money. She mentally shook her head, hoping this didn't turn out to be a waste of her time.

Chloe saw a button that looked like the garage door opener and pushed down hard on the square plastic a few times, but still nothing happened. It was probably the electricity. Perhaps the breaker had been flipped. If not, she'd have to reschedule the showing for when Mr. Henderson returned from his coming trip. That wouldn't be optimal. He was making a special effort to see this house now.

Releasing a sharp sigh of disgust at possibly having to disappoint Mr. Henderson, Chloe started to look for the breaker box, hoping to discover the switch had been flipped to conserve energy. If not, she'd have to make a call to cancel. She couldn't show the house if her client's safety was at stake with the lack of power.

She inched her way around the narrow space in front of the high-profile vehicle, barely able see her hand in front of her face. She certainly didn't relish searching along the wall in the near dark for the breaker box. That was assuming it was in the garage and not the basement.

Chloe, wrapped up in her anger over this lack of electricity, was wholly unprepared for a masked figure dressed in black to pop up from behind the parked vehicle like a specter and thrust a cloth bag over her head. Before she could do more than stand there and let it happen, the intruder pressed the bag against her face as if to smother her.

The claustrophobic fears she harbored kicked in, allowing her arms to swing about wildly in defense. She tried desperately to get the smothering bag off her head as fast as possible. The intruder pressed his hand more firmly on her face, keeping the bag in place, but she stumbled backward, dislodging the bag slightly. She felt a fresh rush of air along her jawline and renewed her efforts to lift the offending material off completely.

The intruder seemed just as determined to keep the bag in place, shoving her harder backwards. She hated moving when she couldn't see a blessed thing. Her shoulder blades hit the back garage wall with a thud as she continued to grapple with the intruder holding the bag still mostly over her head. He pressed into her, sandwiching her between his body and the solid surface of the wall.

In a blind panic, Chloe flailed her arms and kicked her foot in several directions, trying to connect with any part of her assailant. She got a shin or perhaps a knee, it was hard to tell, and her attacker yelped. The pressure of his body against hers lifted momentarily, but it didn't last long.

Together they moved away from the wall, but he squeezed the bag even tighter around her neck in response to her struggling, cutting off the majority of her air. She was soon pushed into the side of the SUV. From a now muffled distance she heard her phone start ringing. It was still in the kitchen by the back door where she'd dropped her purse.

Was Deke calling? He'd be so worried. She should have stayed at his home, like he'd asked her. She'd promised not to show any houses. She'd let her defenses down in light of no threats in the past two weeks. Deke had been right. She shouldn't have let her guard down.

With renewed effort, Chloe kicked out at her attacker again, connecting with what felt like the tire of the vehicle. With a last bit of strength, she bent at the waist and lunged forward, hoping to dislodge her attacker's hold. Instead, she cracked her head on something blindingly hard. Was it the SUV's side-view mirror? A striking flash of pain registered on her upper forehead near the hairline and a trickle of warm liquid spread down her face, trailing into her eye. The blow also zapped her strength quite a bit.

In a last desperate bid for freedom, Chloe sucked in a shallow breath and shrieked as loud as she could. Unfortunately, it sounded too weak to alert anyone but the person already strangling her. Her head crowded with the buzzing sound she knew from limited experience meant she was losing consciousness.

Depraved visions loomed large in her mind, crowding one after another with nightmarish images of the horrendous place she'd wake up in only to face the terror of this man's dreadful whims.

If she ever woke up.

CHAPTER 15

Deke raced to the address Chloe had recited on her message. The places in this neighborhood were very swanky. He wasn't unfamiliar with the area, as many of his clients lived in upscale homes in this neighborhood, but it had been a while since he'd visited.

He almost passed the address, but quickly corrected the steering wheel, one back tire edging over a small corner of the lawn as he made the turn into the driveway. His vehicle sped up the long drive, going through a tunnel-like portico and into the vast parking space behind the house. He saw Chloe's car parked near the back door where a lock box was attached to a wedged-open door. The scene looked dangerous. What if someone had been lying in wait for her? What if someone followed her inside?

Deke drove past her car and wheeled his vehicle around, blocking the better part of three out of the four stalls of the generous garage. He pointed the front of his SUV toward the long driveway exit should he need to leave in a hurry, and threw it into park.

He exited his vehicle, raced across the pavers to the back door. He pushed it open to a large kitchen and yelled, "Chloe!" All he heard was silence for a count of three, then a muffled noise from his right.

"Chloe!" he screamed again, charging toward where he'd heard the noise. He heard the distant sound of a garage door opening and what sounded like a vehicle door slamming shut. He kept moving. It sounded like someone was trying to leave the premises. Deke would stop them.

Through a butler's pantry and down a short hallway, he came to a door. Without regard to his own safety, he slammed it open with his boot applied next to the door handle. The door popped open. Deke saw a ski-masked man seated behind the wheel of a silver SUV. The driver backed the large vehicle out of the garage, or tried to. He wasn't going to make it far. Deke was parked behind him.

Deke didn't see Chloe. He figured Mr. Ski Mask had loaded her into the back of his vehicle somewhere. The guy looked in his direction and suddenly the SUV shot backwards out of the garage, barely clearing the still opening door before slamming into the front quarter panel of Deke's vehicle with a crash.

Bastard.

The guy tried to do a three-point turn to escape, pulling forward and ramming into the garage door's wooden frame before whipping backward to slam into Deke's vehicle a second time. There was no way the guy was leaving with Deke's huge SUV parked at an angle the way it was, no matter how many points he managed to make. But that didn't mean Chloe wasn't in danger of getting hurt in the process.

Deke raced forward as Mr. Ski Mask, who was now wedged between Deke's damaged vehicle the smashed garage door frame, leapt from his trapped vehicle and ran. He disappeared behind a narrow space between the end of the garage and the fence along the back of the parking area.

Deke wanted to follow, but wanted to find Chloe

more. Racing to the driver's door, still standing open from the guy's quick departure, Deke called Chloe's name again. He heard a distinct moan from the back of the bad guy's vehicle, now half out of the garage and firmly wedged against Deke's front quarter panel. He popped the lever that should have opened the back hatch, but it didn't go up very far.

He heard another moan and simply climbed into the front seat, moving between the bucket seats quickly to the back seat. He bent over to look into the rear storage area. It had a vinyl cover he couldn't open from where he was. At least not until he applied his jackknife blade along one edge, slitting it carefully along two edges of the back seat to reveal a small figure dressed in a nice navy suit with a dark hood over her head. The moaning had stopped. She also wasn't moving.

Deke couldn't get the hood off her fast enough. The smear of blood alongside a matted tangle of sleek dark hair made his heart twist with dread and plummet to his knees. Flashbacks of the accident with his ex-girlfriend flooded into his brain as similar images crowded inside.

Blood-soaked tendrils of hair were something he couldn't even watch in movies without traumatic memories engulfing him. Just like they did now. He was too late. Regret threatened to choke him. He took a deep breath, trying to man up and deal with the problem at hand.

"Chloe," he said, trying to get her to rouse. "Please wake up."

He felt under the curve of her jaw for a pulse and exhaled the breath he didn't remember holding when he found a stronger one than expected. He inhaled and exhaled slowly a couple of times, trying to keep his shit together. He grabbed his phone and thumb-dialed 911, asking for paramedics and police in that order, telling them to hurry, which was likely foolish. They always hurried. That's what they did.

Deke pulled several strands of matted dark hair gently from her face, revealing an open injury on her forehead, the likely cause of the copious amounts of blood on her face and in her hair. The memories he tried to hold at bay refused to stay hidden, saturating his brain with vivid recall of what had happened the last time he found himself with a wounded and bloodied woman who had depended on him to keep her safe.

After running Deke's SUV off the road, the cartel assassin had dragged Shelley out of the vehicle, intending to put a bullet in her head as an added measure. Her screams had pulled Deke into consciousness. Thinking Deke was immobilized in the SUV, strapped in and dangling upside down from his seatbelt, the assassin had chosen to taunt him from only a few feet away before killing Shelley.

With blood dripping in his eye, Deke never understood how he made the shot, but it was enough to put the cartel hitman down and keep Shelley alive. She had not been the least appreciative. Shelley blamed him for putting her in danger and promptly exited his life, probably rightly so.

"Chloe," he said. She didn't stir. It took all his willpower not to pull her from the back storage area and cradle her in his arms. He wouldn't move her, in case she had injuries he couldn't see, but put his hand on her shoulder and gripped it gently, wanting to connect and silently reassure her he was there.

"I'm sorry. I shouldn't have left you," he whispered. The massive amount of regret he harbored left a bitter taste in his mouth. "Please hold on. Please come back to me. I promise it won't happen again."

He contemplated what he would do if she was hurt badly. He'd castigate himself mercilessly either way, but he didn't have to think about it for too long because he heard sirens approaching. He kissed his fingertips and placed them against her cheek.

Deke carefully exited the vehicle to direct the paramedics to her. The back hatch was soon wrenched open so they could get her onto a gurney. She moaned when she was moved, but didn't fully wake up, which made him nervous.

They moved her toward the waiting emergency vehicle. Before she was loaded inside, Deke kissed her cheek and whispered in her ear that he'd be there when she woke up. Her pale skin almost matched the white sheet that covered her.

The police asked him lots of questions, which he answered absently, his attention on Chloe being taken care of by the paramedics.

Yes, the masked man likely injured Chloe and stuffed her in the back of the SUV. *No*, there wasn't anyone else here when he arrived. *Yes*, the man looked very much like the one he'd tussled with at Chloe's home a couple of weeks back, but he couldn't swear on it.

Deke surveyed the house, trying to figure out what had happened. What sequence of events had led to this result? Without her account, he was only guessing. The foremost question in his mind was, had the masked guy been waiting for her or had he come in after, following her here when she left the safety of his secure house. The fact that the SUV the intruder tried to escape in was hidden in the garage suggested he'd been hiding inside, waiting for Chloe.

The officer in charge let him go to follow the ambulance to the hospital. Deke headed to the kitchen to retrieve her purse and the car key therein. He'd seen her bag earlier as he'd charged through the kitchen to the garage. Given that his vehicle was damaged, he'd likely have to drive her car to the hospital. Unless they were impounding it for their investigation.

Before he made it two steps in that direction, a fancy town car came through the portico entryway, gliding to a stop in front of the officer directing traffic. The driver's window slid down and a young man poked his head out briefly. The rear passenger door behind the driver opened, and an older gentleman stepped out of the car, concern covering his features as he surveyed the scene.

Even from the distance between them, Deke heard the man ask, "What has happened here? I was supposed to meet my real estate agent. Is she inside?" Before the officer could answer, he asked, "Where is she? Where is Chloe?"

The officer tried to direct him back inside his car, but the older man started walking toward Chloe's car. The chauffeur also exited the town car. Dressed in an ill-fitting uniform that looked two sizes too big, he locked one hand on his opposite wrist and waited at parade rest beside the car, making it clear the officer's instructions were going to be ignored. His focus was on the white-haired gentleman now pointing.

"That's Chloe's car right there," he said in an anxiety-ridden tone. "Please tell me where she is. Where is Chloe?"

The officer in charge motioned for the man to get back into his car, but the guy was having none of it. He continued toward Chloe's car and the back of the house.

Deke intercepted him halfway. "Hi. I'm Deke," he said and stuck his hand out.

The man stopped walking and shook it automatically. "Who are you?" His tone was one of suspicion. "Why are you here?"

Ignoring his questions, Deke asked, "Are you Mr. Henderson, by any chance?"

The man frowned, withdrawing his hand quickly. "How do you know that?"

"Chloe mentioned it when she called me to meet her here."

His bushy gray eyebrows furrowed deeply. "She called you to meet her here? Why would she do that? She was supposed to meet *me* here."

The guy was quite an odd duck. Chloe said he was her richest client. Deke changed the description in his mind. Poor folks were *odd ducks.* The rich were simply *eccentric.*

"I'm her bodyguard. And I suspect she notified me because she was worried about her safety, which turned out to be a good call. Someone tried to abduct her this afternoon. She got hurt."

The man looked at the ambulance pulling through the portico, exiting the property on the way to the hospital. "She's inside there?" he asked absently.

"Yes."

"Will she recover from her injuries?" he asked, turning his gaze back on Deke. The guy had a weird way of putting things. Intelligent, old-fashioned in his speech, yet dressed in expensive clothing and rode around in a town car with a chauffeur, even though the driver needed a better-fitting uniform.

He chalked it up to a general file he labeled, *rich people.* Or perhaps *eccentric people* would be the more apt term.

"That's unclear." Deke stared into the other man's watery, clear blue eyes, wondering how much to share. The urge to say, "She's on her way to the emergency room," died on his lips. He didn't know this guy. No need to give up any more information than necessary.

The man's shoulders suddenly dipped like he was a puppet and his strings had been snipped. "Was it my fault?" he asked in a pitiful-sounding voice.

"I'm not certain. Why do you think you would be to blame?" Did this guy and Deke need to form a club together? He still wasn't certain this fiasco wasn't *his* fault.

Mr. Henderson gestured to the house. "A friend sent me this listing, rightly thinking I'd be interested. I asked Chloe to show me this house today before my business trip. It was a last-minute appointment. But there was a traffic accident and we were a few minutes late. So do you think it was because of me?"

"I can't say," Deke said, feeling a bit sorry for this gentleman and his obviously guilt-ridden feelings. He empathized. "I hope not." *For your sake*.

"Well, this is just very distressing news."

"I'm sorry."

He straightened a little as if trying to bear up and be strong. "I guess it can't be helped. If you talk to Chloe, remind her that I had to leave on my business trip. Also tell her that when I return, I'll get in contact with her and reschedule the showing."

"Sure." Deke went from feeling sorry for the guy to perturbed that his singular concern was about his appointment to see the house being ruined because Chloe had been attacked and nearly kidnapped by a masked intruder.

Mr. Henderson glanced at the house and made a tsking noise. "We'll just have to hope this place is still available when I get back."

Rich people, Deke thought again and subdued the urge to roll his eyes in disdain. It would probably be lost on the guy anyway.

Mr. Henderson started to turn away, but stopped briefly, glancing at the back door. "Did the kidnapper get inside the house and wait for her?"

"That's also unclear." Deke hadn't had a chance to ponder all the intricacies of today's abduction plot.

"Wouldn't the man have to be a Realtor in order to get inside before she did?"

Deke glanced over one shoulder. The guy—rich, eccentric and self-absorbed or not—had a minor point. But then he changed his mind.

"Not necessarily," Deke said, tucking that thought away to check at a later time. "Could have been any number of service people with access to the house. And it could also have been a woman." Chloe's boss came into his head. Was she behind this?

"Perhaps you are correct." He nodded once, a frown firmly in place, but added, "I'll bid you good day then."

Deke nodded once, unsure what reply went with the man's unusual send off. *And to you as well, my good sir,* using his best British accent, perhaps?

Mr. Henderson's town car, driven by his unfashionable chauffeur, exited the property in grand style. Deke turned back to his vehicle, realizing that it was likely not drivable as is. Unsure if the police would let Chloe's car be released from the scene, his shoulders slumped. He'd probably have to call Zak *again* for a ride.

As if conjured from his morose thoughts, the sound of a loud motorcycle in the distance registered and grew louder, as if it was already set to arrive in front of his pitiful stance. Zak cruised through the portico to the back parking area astride his favorite Harley as if he'd been summoned by Deke merely thinking about him. He pulled to a stop in front of Deke, shut the engine off and put his kickstand down.

"Let me guess," Deke said. "You got another alert on your fancy app that I called 911 for the police and another ambulance."

Zak pulled his helmet off and shook out his too-long hair. "Right-o."

"I'd say you're taking an unhealthy interest in my life and tell you to stop it, if it weren't for the fact that I might need a ride."

They both looked at his SUV near the garage, still crushed up against the back end of the masked man's large vehicle. "Bad day?" Zak asked.

"The worst. Let me go see if they'll let me take it, if it's even drivable."

"Why wouldn't they?"

Deke quickly explained all that had gone on with the masked man, Chloe's near abduction and the injuries that resulted in Chloe being unconscious in an ambulance and on the way to the hospital. He wanted to follow to make sure she was okay, but wasn't certain if the police would keep their vehicles as evidence.

Plus, he desperately wanted to be there when Chloe woke up.

Without further discussion, Zak handed him his helmet and keys. "Here. Take my bike and go. I'll take care of all this. You go see about your girl. Call soon and update me."

"Thanks, Zak." Relieved, Deke handed over the keys to his SUV and climbed onto his brother's motorcycle. Quickly fastening the helmet in place, he started the powerful engine up and took off toward the hospital.

He wasn't certain what his next move would be. He only knew he wasn't letting Chloe out of his sight ever again. After spending two weeks living with her, he didn't have the fortitude to revisit the ludicrous notion of never seeing her again or even attempting the stupider idea of a public breakup.

Not long ago, they'd agreed to join forces against any and all foes.

Their greatest foe had just stepped up his or her game. Today's near miss had been calculated. He was called away on a bogus job, and she was lured out of a safe place. What would have happened if he hadn't made it to this address in time? Or if she hadn't told him where to find her?

Deke shook off his foolish what-if angst as useless information to worry over. He revved the engine of his brother's bike, increasing his speed for a faster arrival at the hospital.

CHAPTER 16

Chloe stirred awake to the steady sound of a quiet beep. She opened her eyes and saw a hospital monitor. To her right, the square box on a stand displayed her vital signs, which was what was responsible for making the noise. Clearly, she was in a hospital room. Why was she here?

The memories of her near abduction by the masked man flooded her mind. The steady beep continued, hopefully touting that she was on the mend. There was an IV in her arm and a plastic bracelet on her wrist.

She had a funny taste at the back of her throat. When she tried to move, every place on her body felt bruised.

"Hey, you're up," a familiar voice said from somewhere to her left. Deke stepped into view, a welcome smile on his handsome face.

"Sort of up," she croaked, not even recognizing her own voice. She tried to straighten up, but couldn't manage. He helped her get the hospital bed into a more comfortable position.

"Do you remember what happened?" he asked.

She cleared her throat, but it didn't seem to help her voice when she said, "I remember getting to the house and going into the garage. The power was out. When I went to check the breaker box, a masked man leaped up like the bogeyman and put a bag over my head. I tried to fight him and get the bag off. When I tried to head butt him, I missed and hit something very painful. Everything went black not long after I bludgeoned myself in the fray."

"Must have been scary." He put a hand on her shoulder and squeezed.

"It was." She looked at his worried expression, deeply regretting her actions. "I'm so sorry I left your house, Deke."

He lifted one shoulder and let it drop. "You thought you were only meeting someone you knew and not the bonus guest who showed up. I'm sorry I left you alone."

"You had a job offer. You've spent all of your time the last couple of weeks following me around. You're allowed to work, too."

He shook his head. "Except the job was bogus and when I got there my phone was jammed. I was called away so you could be lured out of the house and knocked out."

Chloe was silent for several seconds before she said, "Our foe almost won that round."

"But he didn't."

"Or she didn't."

He smiled, silently acknowledging her blame of Justine.

"How long *have* I been out anyway?" She was happy to see Deke, but worried, perhaps foolishly, about all that had transpired while she was unconscious.

Deke grabbed a cup with a straw from a nearby table and let her take a sip of water before he answered. "A few hours."

"How many is a few?"

He grinned. "Okay, five hours."

She felt an odd pain and drew her hand up her side to

feel a bandage beneath the hospital gown she wore. "What happened here?"

"He stabbed you with a tranquillizer, too. In fact, it was the same drug that I was given by the masked intruder at your house. Probably even the same guy."

"Bad news."

He pointed to her side and then to his own. "The good news is, now we have matching puncture wounds. The bad news is, the idiot gave you an opiate sedative when you were already knocked out. The doctor wants to keep you here overnight. More good news is that it's already nighttime, so if you go back to sleep soon we can probably leave when you wake up."

Chloe wasn't unhappy to see him here, but wondered how he had all this information. "They told you all that? I figured they'd put up a fuss and call my nearest relative."

"That might have happened, but I told them that we live together. I didn't overstep, did I?" He gave her a lusciously charming smile. If they hadn't already been living together she might have demanded it happen immediately.

"No. You didn't overstep. We do live together. And I like it, by the way." She reached out and held his arm.

"Me, too." Deke drilled her with a devastatingly seductive gaze.

"The truth is, I've been thinking about not wanting to leave your house even after there is no more danger surrounding us."

Deke covered her hand with his. "I've been thinking about that, too. And I'm really glad we feel the same way about it."

She nodded and he pressed a sweet kiss to her lips. "Do you want me to get in touch with your parents, whether or not we live together?"

"No. I don't want my parents involved at this point.

They'd only worry and want me to come to live with them in Florida at their retirement community."

"Perish the thought. Besides, that's way too far away for me to commute."

"Among other issues too numerous to name," she said under her breath.

Chloe tried to sit up higher in the bed. She felt like she was about to slide off the bottom edge onto the floor if she wasn't careful. Deke helped her raise the bed up more. "Did they let you come in the ambulance?"

"No." Deke sighed. "Actually, Zak showed up again when I called 911 for the police and an ambulance."

Chloe laughed. "One of these days your brother is going to say forget it and run far, far away in the opposite direction."

From the door, Zak said, "Not going to happen, gorgeous."

They both looked up as Zak entered carrying a brown paper grocery sack. He reached in and pulled out her purse. "I got it from the house you were showing, but it didn't go with my outfit, so instead of wearing it over one shoulder I just stuck it in this bag and carried it into the hospital instead." He handed the bag to Deke, who stowed it beside her bed under the nightstand.

"Thanks, bro."

"Yes. Thanks, Zak. You're a good sport."

Zak winked at her. "Detective Pullman showed up at the scene and asked me several questions. I told him what I knew, which was nothing, you will likely hear from him again very soon.

"I also took the liberty of driving Chloe's car here. The police released it at the scene since it wasn't a part of the damage to the house. Same with her purse. Good news, since now you'll have both purse and vehicle whenever you leave." He handed Deke her car keys.

Deke reached behind somewhere out of Chloe's line of sight, grabbed a motorcycle helmet and another key, handing it to his brother. "Nice bike. It's very fast."

Zak huffed. "I know. I used to be the *only* one who knew that." He put the key in his pocket and the helmet on the table at the foot of her bed, but a subtle smile shaped his lips.

Deke asked, "And my SUV?"

Zak shook his head, his expression shifting to a discouraged one. "Sorry. They had to tow it." He clapped his palms together, interlocked his fingers, and said, "The front quarter panel is currently melded to the front passenger tire. I'm guessing the Jaws of Life, a blow torch the size of a cannon or possibly both will be needed to part them."

"Where did you send it? Santoro's?"

"Of course. Where else?"

Chloe asked, "Who is Santoro?"

Deke said, "Santoro's Garage is the place we all use for any and all car repair. Rafael Santoro is a genius with all things vehicle related, whether engine repair or body work."

"Good to know," Chloe said, tucking that information away for future reference. She always felt like the word "sucker" was tattooed on her forehead anytime she took her car in for maintenance or repair.

"Anyway, Rafael said it would take a few days, so I got you a replacement car." Zak grinned like a loon. "And it's a hoot."

Deke huffed. "What if I don't want to drive your goofy replacement car?"

Zak shrugged. "I don't give a hoot," he said, chuckling under his breath at his own joke. "The great thing is that you'll be completely incognito. Trust me. No one will recognize you in this POS." Zak promptly popped his brother on the shoulder over her bed. "It's perfect because you never like being the center of attention, Mr. Serious Bodyguard."

Deke gave him a dubious look. "Thanks, bro."

Zak said, "Otherwise, it might be time to consider that safe house, yeah?"

"I'd feel safer holed up in my own secure house."

Chloe pushed out a sigh. "But we can't stay there forever." She promptly sent Deke a soft gaze. "Not that I don't want to, but I hate being tucked away not knowing why this is even happening or what crazy, strange thing is going to happen next."

Zak nodded. "She's right. The escalation and then deescalating were both abrupt. An intruder with a tranquilizer and a gun, then a fairly harmless photo left on your doorstep. Even with the transmitter placed inside the frame of that picture, that's very tame. Then a near abduction with another tranquilizer is quite a leap from both instances. Plus, if you don't figure this out soon, I'm doomed."

"Why?" Chloe asked.

"Of the three of us, I'm pretty sure it's my turn to end up in the hospital next with a large bore needle to the midsection."

Deke looked over Zak's shoulder at the open hospital door and lowered his voice. "Did you get a sample of the drug used on both of us?"

Zak nodded. "I sent it to our favorite FBI agent for analysis and to see if it's been used before and by whom."

"You have a favorite FBI agent?" Chloe asked, her brows narrowing in question.

"Our sister-in-law, Jessica," Zak said. "She's on desk duty right now and typically looking for interesting things to do. She said she'd put a rush on it for us, but it will still take a day or two."

Deke gave Zak a piercing look. "There's something you need to know. I have come to a realization."

"Do tell," Zak said.

"The important conclusion is that I don't believe I'm the target anymore. This can't be cartel related."

"Cartel related?" Chloe's eyes narrowed.

"Long story that I'll tell you later, but suffice it to say, if this had been about me and my past, the intruder wouldn't have abducted you. He would have just shot you—or worse—and left your body for me to find."

Zak said, "Finally, you agree it's not all about you all the time. Miracles can happen."

Chloe shifted in bed. "So we're back to me."

"I'm afraid so. Let's talk about what happened and maybe we can figure out what to do next." Deke asked, "What do you remember about when you went to the house? Did the guy follow you inside when you opened the door?"

"No. He was already inside, parked in the garage and waiting for me."

"His vehicle was already in the garage, too?"

"Yes. I thought it was odd because the home was supposedly vacant, but it wasn't unreasonable to see a vehicle there. Sometimes owners leave things behind until the final sale goes through."

"How did the guy get into the house?"

She shrugged. "Not with me." All of a sudden Chloe remembered Mr. Henderson. "Oh no!"

"What?"

"I was supposed to meet an important client there. I can't believe I forgot about him." Chloe looked around for her purse and phone, knowing it was useless because her client wouldn't answer his cell phone and she couldn't leave a message either.

"Mr. Henderson, right?" Deke asked. She nodded in

surprise. "Don't worry. He showed up by the time you were loaded in the ambulance and was worried about you. He was leaving on a business trip and wanted me to tell you that he'll call you when he gets back to reschedule."

She blew out a semi-relieved breath, grateful not to have alienated her best client with the foolishness going on in her life—unless this was what Justine had planned. Thwarting her efforts with Mr. Henderson was exactly what Justine wanted to do.

Deke turned to Zak. "Any news from the police about a break-in?"

Zak shrugged. "Not while I was there. And it's possible they wouldn't have shared anything with me either way."

"Can you find out?"

"Maybe." Zak shrugged at first and then nodded. "I'll see what I can do to find out any and all pertinent details."

"Anything else you remember?" Deke asked his brother.

"Like what?"

"Did anyone unexpected show up after we left? Someone you thought shouldn't have been there?"

Zak thought for a second then said, "The listing agent showed up there all pissed off because the garage door and the frame around it got damaged by the masked man trying to escape. The guy was frothing at the mouth, wanting to know who was going to foot the bill for repair of the damage. I thought the police were going to have to sedate him."

"The garage was damaged?" Chloe asked, horrified. "Premier Housing might be on the hook for that since I was the one who opened the house."

"Not if there was a break-in before you got there."

"Or if the house was shown earlier by someone

completely unrelated and *they* forgot to reengage the alarm," Zak said.

Deke nodded. "The other possibility that occurs to me was maybe the cleaning service forgot to put the alarm back on the last time they cleaned."

She said, "But if the masked man had broken any window or door before I got there, the silent alarm would have gone off and the police would have beat me there."

"Did you turn the alarms off when you entered?"

Chloe squinted, trying to remember. "No. But I should have had to. The alarm panel was already off when I came inside the kitchen. I forgot all about it until now. Maybe the guy had access to a Realtor code." She sucked in a shocked breath. "What if Justine gave it to him?"

"Wouldn't that make her culpable?"

Chloe frowned. "Yes. But we can call the listing agent and ask who the last agent was that logged in before me. Perhaps there was an earlier showing."

Her phone started ringing shrilly from her purse. Deke retrieved the sack Zak had brought.

"Speak of the devil," Chloe said as she checked the screen to see who was calling, then answered the phone. "What do you want, Justine?"

"What in the holy hell happened today?"

"I was nearly abducted and now I'm in the hospital. That's what happened."

Ignoring what she'd said, Justine practically shouted, "You know the listing agent of that high end home wants Premier Housing to pay for the damages."

"Guess you shouldn't have given the intruder your code to get in."

"I didn't give anyone anything. I certainly didn't open that house up."

"I don't believe you."

"And I don't care what you believe. The only agent that opened the place up in the last week was you."

"Well, someone else was there, because the house alarm was already turned off when I got there."

"Doesn't matter. You have cost me too much already, Chloe. We can't continue like this."

"I agree. I'll take my clients and my current listings and go my own way."

"No. You take nothing, because that's what you came here with."

"That's not true. I came with a handful of clients. Also, Mr. Henderson told me what you did."

"What?"

"He told me you tried to get him to sign a contract with you, but he turned you down, wanting to work with me instead."

"That's crazy. That's not what happened. He came in looking for you and I only—"

Chloe cut in, not wanting to hear any more of her lies. "First you try to pimp me out for sex, then you try to steal my clients and now you're trying to lie and hide from your culpability."

"That's not true," Justine said, but her subdued tone implied the opposite.

"I should put you up before an inquiry board for ethics violations." *That should rile her up.*

There was silence on the line for a count of three. "Try it, Chloe," Justine said. "See what happens."

"I'll take my clients and my current listings, that's what will happen."

Justine said a really bad word and hung up. Chloe hated making such an enemy, but if Justine was responsible for all of this, she had gone way too far.

"That didn't sound good." Deke dropped his hand on top of hers, squeezing as if to comfort her.

"We're done. I'm leaving Premier Housing."

"You're better off."

"Maybe." Chloe was having second thoughts. What if Justine *wasn't* responsible for the intruders or abductors?

"Not maybe. I've seen you at work for the past couple of weeks. Your clients love you and you've never failed to gain an additional one from any of the open houses I've seen you run. If you have your own business, you'd make more money. I believe it."

Chloe looked into his eyes. "Not if I'm locked away in a safe house afraid that every time I stick a single baby toe out into the light, it will be lopped off or abducted or stabbed with tranquilizers. I'm not certain I want to live like a prisoner."

"You're right. Even prisoners get time off for good behavior." Deke smiled and she knew he had a plan. She was so in love with this man.

"What does that mean?"

Zak said, "I want to know what that means, too."

Deke inhaled and exhaled. "Now that I'm certain our foes aren't after me, I believe there are only limited places the threat could be from your world."

Chloe nodded. "Namely Justine and Ned or possibly both of them working together."

"Right."

"So where do we start?"

The doctor—Wishek, the same man they'd seen when Deke had been attacked at her place—came in before Deke could outline his plan of attack. Chloe didn't want to stay in the hospital overnight, but got overruled on that point right out of the gate.

Zak left, not wanting to intrude on her medical visit, telling Deke he'd call him later to discuss any further plans.

Dr. Wishek told them what they already knew regarding the tranquilizer used on Chloe, that is was the same type as what had been used to drug Deke.

"The amount was likely the same dosage, as well."

"What? How come it knocked her out for several hours and me for only a few minutes then?"

"You're bigger than she is and she also had a head injury further complicating things. Comparatively, the two doses were probably the same, just different reactions because of the different body size and weight."

"How long do you estimate the drug would have lasted if she *hadn't* had the head injury?"

"Hard to say exactly." The doctor consulted his pad, staring intently for several seconds and poking the screen a few times.

Deke persisted. "Give me your best guess."

"An hour, maybe two at the most," he said hesitantly.

"When can I leave?" Chloe asked.

"Not until tomorrow morning. Get some sleep."

"I've *been* sleeping," she muttered, but no one seemed to care.

"Any problem if I stay with her tonight?" Deke asked. Chloe hoped he could.

The doctor frowned like he'd just tasted something foul, but shrugged as he poked his forefinger repeatedly on his tablet. "As long as you let her rest."

After reiterating she wouldn't be released until the morning, the doctor left the room.

Deke nodded. "Meaning that first night, I got the tranquilizer meant for you. Probably the gun was for me. But it went over the edge during our brawl on your staircase, so our masked intruder shot me with the drug instead and left because he couldn't use it on you."

"Who wants me tranquilized?"

"Great question. I think we should find out."

CHAPTER 17

"I agree, let's go now," Chloe said, flipping her sheet off.

Deke got a flash of sexy legs and hospital gown. He grabbed for the sheet and covered her legs again, pressing Chloe back to her hospital bed. "We don't need to find out tonight."

She sighed, sinking into the mattress. "But I'd really love to leave."

"I know, but when the doctor isn't playing Candy Crush on his tablet, he seems very knowledgeable."

Chloe laughed. "Candy Crush?"

"I know he's enamored of that tablet he carries around. It can't all be medical stuff, right? I don't begrudge him a game or two now and then."

She brushed his face with her soft fingers. He turned, pressing a kiss to her palm. "You're funny."

"Yes. A hilarious bodyguard, that's me."

"Will you stay with me?"

"I'm never leaving your side again. You'll have to have me surgically removed."

"Okay." He held her hand until she fell asleep, then tucked himself into a chair he moved very close to her bedside.

The next morning, Deke stretched awake after having spent the night not sleeping much in the chair.

Although it had been a long night for Deke, he was so relieved that the cartel wasn't after them he spent his time plotting and planning. He strategized several paths of investigation to discover who their mysterious foe might be, filing them away in his head for later.

After she was released, Deke drove Chloe to his home in her car, using a very convoluted route. He also kept a strict eye out for anyone following them. He didn't see anyone out of place or trying to keep up by the time they got to his gate.

The hoot of a loaner vehicle Zak had ensured made it to Deke's house was a corrosion-laden pumpkin-orange panel van circa the 1970s with more rust visible than paint.

Even the make and model weren't readily discernible, just a big rusty orange bucket of bolts. Deke and Chloe laughed themselves silly over it. He assured her security on a ten-speed bicycle would be more feasible than using the rusted-out "hoot" of a vehicle his brother had left behind.

Once ensconced inside his secure house, Deke took her to bed. He was beyond grateful that he hadn't fucked this all up by continuing to believe that someone was after him.

She started to protest, "I've had enough sleep."

"The nurses woke you up every two hours all night long."

"I slept in between all the interruptions."

Deke grinned. "Good. I'm glad you're rested. I still want you in my bed."

"What if I'm not tired?"

"Even better." Deke moved closer, trapping her against the side of the bed. "Thing is, I don't really want you to sleep during what I hope happens next."

Chloe seemed to relax when his ulterior motives were revealed. "Oh? What did you have in mind?" He leaned in close, kissed her cheek and cupped one breast through the blouse she'd worn the day before. She made an inarticulate noise when his thumb rubbed across one nipple.

"I believe we should get reacquainted, because it seems like a really long time since we got naked together."

"Great idea." Her arms circled his neck and Deke eased her down to the surface of the bed.

"Excellent. Later on, when we've had enough, if that happens, then we can go back to plotting the ruin of any and all foes out to get us. Unless your head hurts too much. Then I'll have to try harder."

"No. I feel great. And I'm in." She smiled deviously. "Or rather, you'll be in, I'll be delighted and I'm sure my head will likely never hurt again."

She tightened her hold around his neck, allowed him to gently pull all her clothing off and soon met him beneath the sheets once he'd shucked off all his clothes, too.

Deke made love to her with the idea that she was precious and he would never let her go. They kissed for half an hour, hugging and touching each other all over before he even sheathed up and entered her warm, slick and still very tight body. Once inside, he made sure to delight her very slowly and methodically. By the sexy sounds she made, he felt like he'd accomplished his seductive goals.

Twice.

When they woke from a sex-induced slumber and started whispering about their plans to defeat all their foes, Chloe said, "I'm glad you realized it wasn't your fault that we were being targeted."

"Me, too. That solution might have involved witness protection."

"Why did you think it was you?"

"Because of what happened with my ex-girlfriend."

"Will you tell me about it?"

Deke told her about Shelley, the accident, the guy who tried to kill her, and why he'd been so convinced he was to blame. He mentioned the guilt was worse because he'd been on the way to break up with Shelley before they'd had the accident.

He even told her he'd convinced himself he shouldn't continue to be in Chloe's life.

"You were planning to break up with me?"

He nodded, but rolled his eyes. "Yes. In a very public way so my foes would ignore you and focus on me. Foolish, I know."

Chloe seemed shocked by the lengths he'd been willing to go. "Why would you ever tell me that?"

"I don't want any secrets between us. I love you. I want to stay with you. I don't want you to ever move out of this house."

She grinned. "I love you, too. I want to stay. While I've enjoyed my place, it was always just my starter home. Your house is like my dream home. Not to mention that you really *do* come with this place, as every woman at my recent open houses wishes were true."

"Yep. For better or for worse, the house and I are a package deal."

She swallowed hard. "Meaning?"

"Oh, I think you know exactly what that means. Do I need to sing a wedding march?"

She squealed in joy, hugging him tight and feeling like they could take on the world if they only did it together.

"I know it's too soon for that song, but I want us to add it to our future plans, okay?"

"Yes. Perfect."

They talked all day, lounging in bed between bouts of

making love and making plans for their future after they solved the mystery of this annoying foe.

Deke talked about his family, both in New Mexico and the vacation place in Key West that they visited twice a year, and about growing up in a houseful of boys. She talked about growing up in Tennessee with her two brothers and how close her parents' house was to Key West.

By midafternoon, Chloe wanted to enact their loosely made plans to vanquish their mysterious foe.

Deke was ready, too.

Chloe crossed her arms. "So Justine or Ned. Who do we go after first?"

Deke lifted one shoulder. "My inclination is to start with your boss, but maybe we should shake things up and go after Ned first. Maybe our foes won't expect that move."

"Excellent. Let's do it."

"Do you have his number?"

Chloe narrowed her gaze. "Maybe."

Deke shook his head. "I'm not accusing you of anything. I just didn't want you to have to call Justine for it. If you did, our other possible foe would be tipped off."

"Okay. Yes. I still have his number. But it's not on my phone. I already deleted it from there when we got back to my house after the game. It's written on a piece of paper in the office desk at my house. And that's only because I've been living here since that night and haven't had a chance to light it on fire and flush the ashes down the toilet."

He smiled at her over-the-top plan to rid herself of Ned's number. "So we need to go to your house?"

She tilted her head to one side as if contemplating something distasteful. "Unfortunately, his phone number is easy to remember, so it's also in my head." She pushed out a dejected-sounding sigh.

"Call him. Ask to meet him on his turf. Don't mention I'm coming with you. We'll let that be a surprise. Okay?"

She nodded. "I'm so grateful we've joined forces."

"Me, too."

Chloe made the call and asked Ned to meet, but was evasive about the subject. He was surprised, but agreed to meet her at his place of business and gave an address.

With Deke's SUV out of commission and the pumpkin panel van Zak had brought truly out of the question as a viable option, they took his sports car. It wasn't as low-key as her sedan, which she offered to let him drive, but he was better acquainted with his sports car. He liked having the opportunity to drive it. When they got to the building where Ned worked and found his office, Chloe seemed shocked to learn he was a property appraiser.

"Didn't he tell you what he did for a living on your big date?"

"No. Early on he mentioned Justine believing we were perfect for each other. Mostly he talked about how he'd spared no expense regarding the tickets he'd bought. Honestly, I thought we'd be in some sky box glass room overlooking the park. I'd pictured a great view and cushy seats without so much close-contact humanity surrounding us."

Deke said, "I've wondered about that. How he got you into the stadium, I mean."

She nodded. "I was really just trying to get along, but I was off my game with all the people around me as we entered the stadium. My focus was on not getting jostled or smothered by all those people.

"By the time I realized where we were headed, it was all I could do to be nice and get to that seat. I was freaked out and trying to calm myself down when you rescued me with an offer of popcorn. And I was profoundly grateful that you didn't push me out of your seat since I was leaning into you so heavily."

"Well, I liked it. You smelled so good I wanted to sniff you like a dog licking his chops and salivating over a juicy morsel. In fact, let me show you what I wanted to do the moment your soft body backed into mine." He kissed her slowly, tenderly, for a long time with lots of agile tongue movements. They were in a public place, so he broke the kiss sooner than he wanted, wishing they were still back at his place.

"I'm so glad we found each other," she whispered.

"So am I." Deke glanced at the listing on the wall again. "I really should send Ned a fruit basket for being such a dick that night and sending you my way."

Chloe looked at the index of offices again. "Yeah, a dick with the power to determine the amount some homes get appraised for."

"How would messing you around impact that?"

She shrugged. "I do have more high-end homes listed than anyone else at Premier Housing. Maybe someone is trying to knock me off the block I've sweated blood to build up the last several years."

"So you think they wanted you kidnapped to steal your listings?"

She shrugged. "I have no idea. But it's the first thing that comes to mind if Justine is involved. As owner of Premier Housing, she'd get first pick of all my listings if I left without them."

They stepped into the elevator. "What do you want me to ask him?"

"Why don't I do the talking?" He pushed the appropriate numbered button.

"Even better," she said as the elevator whisked them upward.

Ned opened his office door to see her centered in it. Deke waited out of view to one side.

"Chloe," Ned said, his voice sounding as oily as Deke remembered. "Come on in. It's just you and me. I sent my assistant home for the day."

Chloe walked through the door. "Why?"

He frowned. "I thought you wanted to kiss and make up. Who knows where that will lead us? I certainly didn't want to get interrupted if that was the case."

Deke slid in right behind Chloe before Ned could close the door. "Too bad that's not going to happen."

"You!" Ned turned an accusatory stare on Chloe.

Deke shoved Ned back a step and closed the door himself. "So sorry, you piece of shit. She only kisses me now and she doesn't want to make up with you. We're not here for that."

"What's going on? Why *are* you here?"

"We want to know what the fuck is going on between you and Justine."

"What?" Ned blanched. "I don't know what you're talking about." He definitely knew something.

"You're lying." Deke and what he considered his intimidating height towered over Ned. "Spill it already or I'll help you."

To say the guy sang like a canary wasn't far off in either what he said or the pitch of his voice when he tattled all he knew.

"It was for the money, okay?"

"Explain." Deke leaned in. "And use lots of details."

Ned's hands came out in front as if to shield his body. "Justine was losing high-end clients to Chloe. Apparently, she has a special rapport with several of the richer clients and they all talk to each other."

He paused and swallowed hard.

"Go on," Deke prompted.

Ned closed his eyes, took a deep breath, opened them and continued. "Once a member of that elite circle vouches for you, they don't want anyone else. All the new high-end clients were coming to Premier Housing, but asking specifically to deal with Chloe. Justine used to be the one the rich clients asked for, but now it's Chloe. If that trend continued—and it would have—it was only a matter of time before Chloe started making more than Justine or went off on her own, taking all her high-end clients and their friends with her. At least that's what Justine believes."

"So why try to abduct me?"

Ned's eyes rounded to perfect circles. "Abduct you? I never did that! I wasn't part of anything like that. I got us expensive game tickets to woo you into bed. That's it."

"Why? What was the plan?"

Ned shrugged. "Once I'd nailed you a couple times, the idea was to have me do a few of your appraisals because you'd want to scratch my back like I'd scratched yours. I'd do the appraisals and up the prices so the clients you had were paying more at closing. It's not like they negotiate. You tell them a number and they pay it. That's all. The next part was to have Justine come in and question the prices, like they were too high."

"So if Chloe's clientele thought they were being cheated, they'd go back to Justine." Deke pondered the idea that if Ned didn't know anything about Chloe's abduction—and he seemed truly shocked by the idea of a kidnapping plot—perhaps Justine was working with someone else.

"I don't understand why Justine would do that." Chloe crossed her arms, her brows furrowed. Deke wanted to kiss her senseless and smooth her worries away. But he should focus.

Ned shrugged. "Justine used to have all the premium houses before you came along. Slowly but surely over the past several years you've gained the majority. She used to rant about it whenever we were together, at work or not."

Deke glanced at Ned. "You're sleeping with Justine."

He turned red, started shaking his head and stammered, "Well...I...not...we..."

"Never mind, I get it. Don't hurt yourself."

Chloe cut her gaze to Deke and shook her head at the idea of Justine and Ned sleeping together. How deranged must Justine be to send her lover off to have sex with another woman for the purposes of ruining her client base in the real estate market? "But Justine gets a cut of every sale I make."

"Not as much as if the clients were all still hers," Ned said. "So she promised to cut me in for half of whatever extra she made. But that's it. No kidnapping needed, right?"

Ned's phone started ringing. He looked at his screen and said, "Speak of the devil."

"Don't answer that," Deke said to Ned.

Just as soon as the last note sounded on his phone, Chloe's phone started ringing. "Surprise. It's Justine," she said. Turning to Ned, she asked, "Did you tell her I was on my way over here?"

Ned made a face like a pouty little child caught with his hand in the cookie jar and shrugged defiantly. "Maybe. Maybe not." *Which means yes. Bastard.*

Deke fisted his hands, wanting to punch this loser so much his knuckles ached with desire.

"Answer it," he told Chloe.

It was time to start their own devious plan.

Chapter 18

Chloe was still processing her shock and outrage over Justine and Ned being in cahoots. "Answer it and say what?"

"Tell her you're on your way over to talk to Ned. She doesn't have to know we're already here. Also tell her you want to see her later today. Pretend you're trying to make nice." Deke seemed to have a plan. She'd go along, trusting him with all her heart.

She nodded, answering the call with a subdued, "Yes."

Justine's patented hard-core bitch tone came through the line loud and clear. Deke likely heard it from where he stood.

"Heard you were on your way over to Ned's," Justine barked.

Chloe pulled the phone away from her ear an inch and said, "That's right."

"Why?"

Chloe closed her eyes. "I've been thinking about a few things after my brush with danger yesterday. Perhaps I was rash the last time we spoke. Maybe I'm making amends." *Liar, liar, pants on fire.*

That seemed to calm Justine. "What do you mean?"

"I'm not ready to go out on my own just yet, Justine. I'd like to talk to you later, if you're available. Are you in the office right now?"

"Yes. I am here in the office, but I have an appointment scheduled in a few minutes. In fact, my client just arrived." It sounded like Justine put a hand over her phone to say, "I'll be right with you," to someone. Then she was back. "How about we meet here in an hour, Chloe? I should be finished up by then. We can discuss our continued working relationship."

"Fine. Good." Chloe inhaled deeply and said, "Thank you."

Justine hung up without further sentiments.

"She wants to meet in an hour to discuss our continued working relationship," Chloe said to Deke. "She's with a client right now."

"Okay. Let's go," he said. "We can be there in less than twenty minutes to surprise her before her client leaves." Deke turned to Ned. "What do I need to threaten you with to keep you quiet?"

"Nothing. I'm staying out of this from now on. Tell Justine she's on her own. I don't know who else she's in bed with or what they're planning and I don't want to know. I'm out. You can tell her that for me."

They took the elevator back down again. Deke tried to call his brother to ask if he'd heard from their sister-in-law about the drug used on them and where it might have originated.

"Damn it," he said after a couple of seconds.

"What?"

"No signal." He held his phone to each of the four corners of the elevator, to no avail apparently. He muttered a few swear words under his breath.

"Maybe once we get out of this building, you'll have a signal."

"Or there's a signal jammer around here somewhere,

like the one used to lure me away from you yesterday."

"Is that likely?"

"No. Some buildings are just less forgiving where cellular signals are concerned. Just because we had a signal in nimrod's office doesn't mean that translates to the rest of the structure."

When they got out of the elevator and into the parking garage, Deke's phone still couldn't get a signal. He uttered a few more creative swear words under his breath, which made her smile. The moment he drove out of the parking structure under the building, his phone came back to life.

So did Chloe's. Her phone chimed, signaling a text.

"Did you miss a call?"

"No. It's a text from Justine. That's kind of strange. She just told me she had a client walking in the door."

"What's the message?"

Chloe read it out loud. "Just learned something you need to know."

"That's it?"

She nodded.

"Cryptic."

"Yes. And it means she's playing with me. Ned called her the instant we left his office to rat us out. She's learned we've discovered her secret and are about to confront her."

"You could be right. But that's okay. Now we know what she's up to."

"Maybe. She's probably going to demand I hand over my office keys and give me a sad little cardboard box to carry all of my personal items. I may be on my own after today."

"I'll carry your box for you. And I still say you'd do fine without her. Apparently she thinks so too if what Ned told us is to be believed."

"Maybe," she said, staring out the window for several

minutes as she thought of all the possible sudden changes to her career.

Chloe still struggled with the depth of Justine's machinations with Ned. The clear picture from Ned that he and Justine had been sleeping together made her sick at heart.

Could it be true? For the life of her, she couldn't think past the reason Justine would do it. She and her boss had their differences, but it seemed out of character for Justine to sink so low.

Deke asked, "What?"

"I don't know. Something feels wrong."

"It all feels wrong."

"No. I mean I feel like I'm missing something."

"Like what?"

"I don't know. I just have a weird feeling about Justine's motives. She's never been a cut her nose off to spite her face sort of person. But I can't think of any other reason she'd scheme with Ned the way she did. I feel like perhaps something else is going on."

"Take it from me. Gut feelings can be overrated. Until yesterday, I was convinced a cartel was after you because of something I'd done long ago."

Chloe smiled at him. "I still appreciate that you worried about me."

"I always will."

Chloe put her hand on his thigh, which he covered with his fingers and squeezed.

"Don't worry," he added. "We won't leave Justine's office until she spills her guts. Answer her back. See if she explains further."

Chloe texted Justine. *So what did you learn? What was your message about?*

There was no response. Chloe tried to call her, but it went to voice mail. She didn't leave a message. They'd be there in a few minutes. They'd also be well over thirty minutes early. If Ned hadn't called and told her when they left, maybe she'd be surprised.

The front door to the realty office was unlocked, but it didn't look like the place was open. It was dusk. The lights had been turned down to only the ones left on after closing.

They entered the shadowy office, Deke slightly ahead of Chloe. She pointed to the light down the central hallway, whispering because it seemed appropriate in the empty space. "An office light is on. Could be either mine or Justine's."

"Justine's office is next to yours?" Deke asked in a low tone.

She nodded.

They walked slowly down the hall past the open reception area.

"Justine?" Chloe raised her voice, which echoed down the hall. Nothing.

At the end of the central hallway was a T. Straight ahead were two conference room doors, one on the right and the other on the left with glass walls except for the partition that divided the two rooms. Many of the walls inside Premier Housing were clear and see through, but not all of them.

To the right, past the conference rooms, a short hallway led to both Justine's office and Chloe's right next to it. The lights in Justine's office were on.

To the left was another short hallway leading to an empty office, the bathroom and an exit.

Chloe approached Justine's office with a bit of trepidation. She couldn't see the other woman from the door, but perhaps she'd gone to the rest room or stepped across the street for a cup of coffee. Unlikely, since she'd left the front door wide open. It was after business hours and a bit spooky.

"Where is she?"

"Don't know," Chloe said. "Bathroom, perhaps?"

"Want to wait in her office?"

"No. Let's wait in mine. We'll see her come back."

Chloe moved into her office, flipping the overhead light on as she stepped inside her space. Once the lights blinked on, she noticed right away that a file cabinet she usually kept locked was not only unlocked but the top drawer was open slightly.

She strode over, yanked out the drawer and flipped through the folders to see if any were missing. She didn't notice anything immediately, but if someone had taken any individual papers out of the folders, it wouldn't be readily apparent. It might take her months to discover what was missing.

"What's up?" Deke asked.

"This is supposed to be locked." She glanced at her desk. It looked like things had been moved, as if someone had searched the surface. "And someone was at my desk moving things around."

"What could they get?"

"Client files mostly. Nothing too secret, but I hate the idea of Justine rifling through my desk for anything."

"Not to defend her, but it could have been someone else."

"Who?"

He shrugged. "I don't know. Just leaving our options open. What if someone broke in here instead of Justine?"

"How would I know that?"

"Go look in her office and see if anything looks out of place or if her file cabinet is open."

The wall she shared with Justine was not glass, so they actually had to go into the woman's office to do as Deke suggested.

Chloe walked the few short steps to the threshold of Justine's office. Nothing looked out of place, but there was a file on her desk with a single sheet of paper on top. From the door, it looked like a consent form. One step closer and a deep lean forward, and she saw that it was a private consent form, filled out but unsigned. The name at the top of the form was easily read even upside down.

Edgar Henderson.

Maybe Mr. Henderson had changed his mind and wanted to meet with Justine after the fiasco at the house showing where Chloe had been attacked. She'd never even seen him that day, though Deke had told her Mr. Henderson was worried about her and promised to get in touch once he returned from his business trip.

Beyond the far edge of Justine's desk, Chloe also saw something disturbing. A single shoe, on its side as if left behind in a rush. Why would Justine leave a shoe behind? Was the other one kicked off behind the desk out of sight from its mate? Where could she have gone without her shoes?

Chloe walked around Justine's desk. She was completely unprepared to see the other woman sprawled on the floor beneath her desk, not moving, the matching shoe half off her other foot.

Suppressing the urge to scream, she inhaled deeply in utter shock.

Justine! Oh no.

Deke stood in the doorway of Justine's office with his attention behind him, wanting to keep anyone lurking around in the office from sneaking up on them. At Chloe's sharp intake of breath, he strode to join her and saw a woman on her side crumpled in the foot well of the desk. Her blouse was untucked. The lower edge of the fabric rode halfway up her back. He could see a small spot of blood on her skin.

"This is Justine?" he asked.

"Yes."

Chloe stepped aside as he squatted down to see if Justine was alive. Her pulse seemed slow to him, but at least it was there.

"Call the police," Deke told her. "But don't use the desk phone. In fact, don't touch anything else if you can help it."

"Is she alive?"

"Yes, but her pulse is weak." He got a better look at the spot of blood on her back. She hadn't been shot. Upon closer inspection, it looked more like a puncture wound. There was slight swelling around it. It looked more like an ice pick wound than a needle mark, unless the syringe had come with a really big, needle. He shivered at the thought.

"I see some blood on her back. It's too small to be a bullet, but it could be a syringe wound with a large bore needle. Tell them she might have been drugged."

Chloe retrieved her cell and made the call, mentioning the syringe wound and the doctor they'd both had at the hospital. It seemed like forever before anyone arrived. The police came in first, herding them into the central hallway so the paramedics could get inside to care for Justine.

The lead investigator, Detective Pullman, pulled them aside for questioning. "The operator said you mentioned Ms. Keller-Howe had been drugged. How did you know?"

Deke said, "I guessed because Chloe and I suffered similar wounds in the past several weeks."

"We were both seen by Dr. Wishek," Chloe added. "He can confirm what we've said."

"Okay. Were you meeting the victim here?"

"Yes."

"Can you tell me the nature of the meeting?"

Chloe's mouth opened and closed. She looked at Deke as if afraid to elaborate on her possibly being fired and the circumstances of Justine being unconscious.

Deke said, "They were meeting here to discuss work."

Pullman's brows narrowed. "Is that so? Can you be more specific?"

Chloe cleared her throat. "I'm thinking about going out on my own. We were going to discuss the specifics of me leaving this brokerage."

"Oh?" He seemed surprised she was candid. "Any hard feelings with this split?"

She shrugged. "Maybe. It's difficult to go out on your own, but I've been here long enough and it's time."

They all three watched as Justine was loaded up on a rolling gurney and taken out to the ambulance.

Deke was convinced more than ever that the attacks centered on Chloe. It was a huge relief that he hadn't brought this down on her head, but he worried about who out there was after her.

With Ned and Justine seemingly innocent at this point of the abductions, Deke wasn't certain what their next step should be. They might have to wait until this phantom made his or her next move. And he hated waiting around for some threat to react to—even though it was the very nature and practice of being a bodyguard.

If Chloe had been Deke's client instead of the woman he'd fallen head over heels in love with, he'd have already advised her to leave the area. He also would have scheduled a trip for them both to go someplace she'd never been before.

Pullman seemed thorough and very motivated to solve these crimes, telling them he'd sent samples of the mystery drug out for analysis, but hadn't heard anything back yet. Neither had Deke from his FBI family source, Jessica. He knew Zak would call the moment he knew anything.

A uniformed police officer came in carrying a woman's purse in gloved hands.

Chloe pointed to it and said, "That looks very much like the purse Justine uses regularly."

Pullman asked the officer where it was found.

"It was in the Dumpster out behind the building. Looks like the wallet and phone are missing, but there were several business cards inside with the name Justine Keller-Howe and some personal items."

"Then that's Justine's purse," Chloe said glumly.

Deke knew exactly what she was thinking. Justine might have tried to steal some clients and undermine her professionally, but she didn't deserve to be accosted in her office because of it. Deke agreed. Someone had an agenda, but had hidden it well thus far. They needed a break.

"This isn't your fault," Deke whispered when the detective and officer moved a few steps away to talk.

Chloe's phone rang before she could say anything. "Yes," she answered politely. After listening to the caller for a few moments, she said, "I am? Really? Uh huh. Okay. Yes. I'll be right there."

"What's up?" Deke asked.

Her brows furrowed in that cute way she had when trying to figure something out. "That was the hospital. I never knew this, since it's never come up before, but apparently I'm Justine's emergency contact. They want me to head to the hospital because she's in the ER about to be moved to the ICU and they want to talk to me about her treatment."

"I'll admit I did not see that coming."

The investigator overheard their discussion of Justine. He released them for the time being. He had a few more questions, but said he'd catch up with them at the hospital to finish the interview.

On the drive over to the hospital, Deke and Chloe

talked about who could be doing this and the bigger question of why.

"If it's not Ned or Justine, then I'm not certain where the threat is from," Chloe said.

"I agree with you. It's a difficult predicament."

"What do you think we should do next? For example, what if you were my bodyguard?"

"If you were my client and not the girl I'm madly in love with, I'd tell you to take a trip out of the country on a private jet and hide away from the world for a while, maybe even in a tropical getaway with no extradition. In fact, it's the same thing I'd tell the girl I'm madly in love with, too."

Chloe snapped her fingers, as if chagrined over a missed opportunity. "So sorry. My private jet is in the shop for maintenance and cleaning. What else do you have?"

"In a couple of months my parents will be vacationing down in Key West at their other home. We could hide down there, but only for a couple of weeks. Plus my four brothers are usually there at the same time, too. Good news, you've already met two of them. Bad news, it's a houseful and even though my brothers would protect you, it's a foolish place to try to hide."

"Sounds interesting, but I'd also hate to bring the heat of the tranquilizer-wielding phantom abductor down on your family's heads, especially during their vacation. It's not good manners where I come from."

"Decent of you to worry about them, but I promise they can all take care of themselves. Dare I say that the brothers Langston are a bunch of bad boys? We rarely worry about any foes. We just get together and kick ass as needed."

"Sounds awesome. But still, I'd like to at least identify the phantom before inviting him on vacation with your parents and your brothers, whether or not they are all bad boys who kick ass, and I have no doubt they are exactly what you say they are."

Deke parked in the covered parking garage attached to the hospital and escorted Chloe inside. Once on the correct floor, Chloe was called into Justine's room to discuss her condition, but he wasn't allowed in with her.

He kissed her cheek before she entered. Under silent protest, he prowled back and forth along the hallway, waiting for her to come back out. The only reason he didn't fight their separation was because there was a window and he had eyes on her.

Before he had time to get bored, his phone buzzed with a call from Zak. The busy nurse at the desk took the time to frown at him as he answered it, so he walked a few steps down the hallway, out of her line of sight.

"Hey," Zak said. "I'm at Premier Housing. Where are you?"

"I'm at the hospital with Chloe. What are you doing at Premier Housing?"

"Did she get hurt again?" his brother asked, ignoring his question and obviously very concerned.

"No. Sorry to mislead. Her boss was attacked. It's possible she was also stabbed with a tranquillizer. How did you get to Chloe's office?"

"Given the trouble you've been having of late, I took it upon myself to load Chloe's phone number into my new app, notifying me of any 911 calls she makes, too."

Deke shook his head, uncertain whether to be relieved or concerned that his brother was such a nosey guy. Before he could comment, Zak said, "I'm coming to you."

"Why?"

"Jessica called with information you need to hear. Call her and I'll be at the hospital in a few minutes so we can discuss any plans of action."

Deke walked a few steps along the hallway, glanced

inside to see Chloe still talking to Dr. Candy Crush about Justine's condition. Even through the window and from several paces away, they both looked dour.

Pullman arrived a few minutes later, nodded at him once and stepped into the room with Chloe and the doctor. Deke walked a little further down the hall, well away from the frowning desk nurse. He had eyes on the room's door, but with the detective in there with Chloe, he felt like she was in good hands since he wasn't going to be allowed inside no matter how sinister he made his expression.

He dialed Jessica's work number. "Hey. I heard you had information for me."

His sister-in-law said, "I do. Thanks for the excitement."

"You sound tired."

"Yeah. It turns out that growing a new human, even a small one, takes quite a lot of energy."

"I've heard that." Deke's brother, Reece, was a very lucky man to have not only Jessica but also a little Langston on the way.

"We finally identified the mystery substance you sent us. It's actually an older synthetic drug manufactured and used more readily about thirty years ago. These days only a handful of places use it, which as you know makes the search easier. I then narrowed it down to only one place that has ordered it in the last year."

"Because you're awesome. Who still uses it?"

"It's a research place. The most recent note said they were conducting a special study, but they've been ordering this particular drug regularly for a couple of decades."

"Got a name for me?"

She laughed. "Come on, Deke. It's never as easy as that. The company in question is owned by yet another company that in turn is owned by someone else. The third company turned out to be a shell corporation, but I managed to stumble across the name of an actual person from over twenty years ago who used to sign for the shipments way back then. No telling whether they still even work there."

"Give it to me anyway. Maybe I can track this mythical person down," Deke said without enthusiasm. He expected a twenty-year-old signature to be a useless avenue, but better than nothing at all. He might yet be surprised.

Jessica said, "And the winner is, Mr. Edgar Henderson."

CHAPTER 19

Chloe entered Justine's hospital room with a lump in her throat, guilt choking her emotions. They wouldn't let Deke in with her, but he kissed her cheek and promised he'd wait just outside the door.

Dr. Wishek waited, electronic tablet in hand, a serious expression shaping his young features.

"How is she?" Chloe asked.

"Justine's condition is listed as serious but stable, but she's also been drugged with the same mystery concoction you and your boyfriend were given."

"Why is she in such serious condition versus our experience?"

"She had a higher dose of the drug, almost double the amount, in fact. This level of the drug would have probably taken your boyfriend down for a few hours, but in Justine's case it's a very dangerous level. She's in a coma. I'm not sure when or even if she'll wake up at this point. But naturally we'll hope for the best. Once the drug wears off, she could have a full recovery. We're just in the waiting stage right now."

Before Chloe could approach the bed, Detective Pullman stepped inside the room to question the doctor.

He told Chloe he'd talk to her later if he needed anything more from her.

Chloe walked to Justine's bedside and entered the curtained cocoon. Without touching the other woman, she bent down to whisper her sympathies over her injury. The nurse, bustling around the small space, checking on the fluids and machines attached to Justine, looked like she wished Chloe would leave immediately.

The sound of her phone in her purse making a loud *ding*, signaling a new text, made the nurse's frown even deeper.

Retrieving the offending device seemed to make the nurse more hostile. She lifted one rigid arm and pointed to a slit in the curtain right next to the bed. "There's a bathroom in the corner over there," she said tersely. Her unspoken message seemed to be, *if you are so rude as to leave your phone on, listen to your messages in there.*

Chloe quickly stepped through the curtain and opened the door to the bathroom. A message from Deke number popped up on her phone's display.

Can't use my phone in here.
Meet me in the parking lot.

Odd. They didn't text much. Deke said he preferred hearing her voice, even if only for a short call. Maybe a nurse had given him a terse look, as well.

She peeked through the door with the idea she'd tiptoe through Justine's room to get out, but heard a noise behind her from the room that shared the bathroom.

"Chloe," came a masculine whisper, almost too quiet to hear. Was it Deke? She pushed the door to the next room wide, but didn't see anyone.

She stepped over to the partially open curtain, seeing an empty bed through the gap, but then the curtain came to life. A gloved hand shot out from the opening toward her face. A damp cloth was smashed over her mouth and nose. She was grabbed up in a tight-armed embrace. She tried not to inhale as she kicked and flailed, but was slowly losing that fight as her body screamed for air. Pushing her last little bit of air out, she tried not to breathe more in.

Chloe would have continued to struggle, but fumes from the cloth smashed against her face made their way into her system. She felt dizzy. As her consciousness faded and she knew she was about to black out, Chloe tucked away a little piece of anger.

If she woke up, or rather when, the person responsible might get an earful before they did whatever they'd worked so hard to accomplish. She'd be quite a handful once she got a chance.

She had one last spark of awareness. Her brain cried out to the man she loved. The man who hadn't sent her a text and who'd be very angry once he found out she was gone. She took solace in the fact that Deke wouldn't stop until he found her. He loved her. She loved him. He would come for her.

Deke's beautiful face filled her mind, and then it was lights out.

Deke stood up straight the moment he heard Henderson's name. "Repeat that name, please."

"Edgar Henderson," Jessica said. "Next to his signature is the title Lead Research Lab Technician. Do you know him?"

"I do know him. He's one of Chloe's clients."

"Chloe? Is she the girl you kissed at that baseball game?" Jessica's voice had lowered to a whisper.

"How do you know about that?"

"You do know that your brothers all gossip like old women, right? I'm certain you have also been a part of this honored tradition in your family."

Deke wasn't willing to admit to any gossip with his brothers, asking instead, "What do you know?"

Her voice lowered even further. "Well, I heard Reece talking to Alex about the picture someone left on your doorstep. He mentioned that it was a framed photo of you kissing a girl at a baseball game. Of course, I'm anxious to meet her."

"What else?"

"Zak says he's met her several times. He says she's very nice and seems to like you a lot, which he pretends surprises him, because brothers all give each other shit about everything, especially romances. Trust me, I know this." Reece's, wife was the youngest of five and the only girl in her family growing up. Jessica knew what she was talking about with regard to brothers and how they behaved.

"I have no doubt you do."

"When do I get to meet her?"

"No comment." Deke ignored the information about him and Chloe spreading like wildfire through the branches of his family tree, and asked, "Don't suppose you have a current address on Henderson do you?"

He heard a ping on his phone, signaling a message had arrived before he even finished asking his question.

"Everything I have on Henderson, the companies he worked for listed along with the shell company in question. Also his address from twenty years ago, and the most recent house he purchased is in the file I just sent to your phone."

"Thanks, Jessica."

"Sure. I enjoyed the challenge. If I find anything else relevant, I'll forward it to you."

"I owe you."

She laughed. "Maybe you can bodyguard my baby one of these days."

Deke hadn't spent much time around little kids or babies, but looked forward to the challenge.

"Maybe," he said evasively.

"Or you could spill everything about this girl you're in love with."

Deke snorted over the phone. "Not likely," adding a quick, "See ya later."

Jessica laughed. "Bye, Deke."

Deke stifled a smile regarding his family knowing about Chloe. He did love her. He'd probably take her to the next family gathering in Key West in a couple of months.

He opened the file Jessica had sent, wondering what Henderson was up to. Chloe was going to hate hearing about this. The only company in the land using a decades-old drug was associated with her richest client.

Deke's mind flew to Henderson's possible motives. What was the guy after? Duh. Chloe. She'd always been the answer.

Now he just needed to know whether Henderson wanted her dead or alive. That wasn't really accurate. He needed to retrieve her from the hospital room, escort her out of this hospital to a secret place far, far away. He'd start by sending a call out to his brother regarding the safe house and get that set up for later tonight.

He sent another text to get that ball rolling and saw the doctor exit Justine's room.

"Doctor," Deke said. "Is Chloe still talking to the detective?" He glanced through the window, expecting to see her, but didn't. Was she behind the partly open curtain? He saw someone moving around by the bed.

Dr. Wishek looked up from his tablet briefly. "No. They both left already, I think."

"What? You think? Where is she?" Deke moved to

the door to Justine's room intending to enter. He didn't care if he wasn't invited. He pushed the heavy door open.

The doctor followed him. "You really can't be in here, Mr. Langston."

"Chloe?" Deke said in an over-loud voice.

A nurse violently opened the curtains, revealing Justine's unconscious form. "Shh," she said with a finger across her lips in the universal sign of be quiet. "Visiting hours are over," she added.

"Where is Chloe?" he asked, prepared to go toe to toe with her.

The nurse pursed her lips. "The woman who was in here before?"

He nodded, knowing he didn't have time to be nice, but had to play by someone else's rules for the moment.

She pointed to a door near the corner of the room. "Her phone made a noise and she went into the bathroom to answer it."

Deke moved in that direction. "How long has she been in there?"

"I have no idea," the nurse said, although she didn't sound too broken up. "My focus was on my patient, where it should be."

He pushed through the curtains and knocked loudly on the door, noticing it was open a crack. "Chloe?" he said, nudging the door wider.

The bathroom was empty.

Panic didn't set in until he noticed another door leading to a connecting room.

"Chloe?" he said louder, going into the next room, not caring if anyone was in there.

He flung the curtains aside. There wasn't even a bed in here. He turned, raced to the room's other exit and out into the hallway. To his left, around a corner and through some doors marked *hospital personnel only*, was where he'd been waiting earlier while talking to Jessica.

Where he stood now was supposed to be only hospital people. So his foe was likely dressed in scrubs or hospital whites. It would be difficult to discover who had Chloe unless he saw her.

To his right were two elevators. He scanned the numbered lights above the doors. One elevator was going up and the other was going down. Neither was headed to this floor. *Fuck*. This was bad. This was so bad.

His phone rang. It was Jessica again.

"What's up?"

"Something just caught my eye when I did a little further research that I thought you should know. The shell company I sent you before has a private jet listed in its holdings."

"Okay. What should I know about that?"

"They just filed a flight plan headed out of the country from an airport here locally. Seemed coincidental, you know?"

"Yes. You're right. Which local airport?"

"Baxter's Airfield, north side of town. It's scheduled for departure within the hour."

This is so fucking bad. Deke had to close his eyes to keep the panic from making him useless. Baxter's was a hike across town. Chloe had been gone for as much as fifteen or twenty minutes already. A sizable head start. What if he couldn't make it to her in time?

"What's wrong?" Jessica asked. "What's so fucking bad?"

Deke was so wound up he hadn't realized he'd spoken out loud.

"Chloe's missing." Deke looked down, seeing something in his periphery. "I've got to go, Jessica." A small, square black item was on the floor next to the door he'd just come out of.

It was a phone. He picked it up. Turning it over, he looked at the display.

Fuck. Chloe's phone. The screen had a message from him telling her to meet him in the parking lot. But he hadn't sent a message.

This was so bad. The time stamp was over fourteen minutes ago. An eternity if he was playing catch up. And he was.

Chloe stirred, but didn't open her eyes. She took stock of herself first. She was in a vehicle. She remembered immediately that she was in trouble. She'd been manhandled and drugged unconscious by someone hiding in the room next to Justine's. The masked man had perhaps finally caught up with her and won this round.

How had their foe known she was at the hospital? Perhaps it was the person who'd assaulted her boss and put her in a coma with yet another syringe. Maybe he'd been lurking around Premier Housing, waiting to follow Chloe. Thinking about the place where she'd been taken also made her remember who'd been waiting for her out in the hall.

Deke. She knew without a doubt that he'd start looking for her the moment he realized she'd been taken. He'd also blame himself for not being allowed in Justine's room with Chloe. She'd been taken from the adjacent room, well out of sight of where he'd positioned himself in the hallway to keep an eye on her. In trying to keep from breathing in the substance on the cloth that had already been making her dizzy, she hadn't made much noise in the struggle.

Surely by now he realized she was missing. How could he ever find her? *She* didn't even know where she was. The idea of never seeing him again brought too much anguish to bear, so she refocused her attention and growing anger elsewhere, directing it at the person responsible.

She'd finally discover what in the world was going on. Too bad the price of solving this mystery might end up being her life. This was the part where she should likely wish she'd listened to Deke and his plan to spirit her away to a tropical locale and a life not resembling the one she'd built for herself in any single way. The notion, while nice in a dreamy, fantasy sort of way, also fortified her anger. She chose her life and some stranger was trying to bend her to his will.

The sway of the vehicle was rhythmic. They must be on a highway and not in the stop and go traffic of downtown. Chloe opened her eyes slowly. They focused on a crystal decanter atop a small bar with stout glasses and other bottles of liquor. What kind of car was this?

Her eyes opened wider. She saw carpet on the floor. It looked like a limo, much like the one she'd ridden in the first night she met Deke. She was resting on the seat, slumped over on her side.

Chloe slowly moved, turning her head and hoping she wasn't about to see Deke's friend Garrick. Her blurry vision focused on a man in a business suit at the back of the limo talking into a cell phone. It looked very familiar to that scene after the baseball game.

She squinted. Was it Garrick? Her gaze cleared and she saw her foe distinctly. Nope. Not him.

Chloe wasn't prepared for it. He was the very last person she ever would have expected as a foe.

Mr. Henderson, her very best client.

Seated next to him was the man she knew as his driver, Klaus. They were all inside a limo, not the town car Mr. Henderson usually rode around in. The vehicle was moving, so someone else must be driving. Klaus must have gotten a promotion to henchman.

The anger she remembered was about to boil over and cover Mr. Henderson. How had she not had even an inkling that he was behind this?

"There you are, Chloe," he said with a smile, like nothing was amiss. "I knew I had the dosage right this time." *This time?*

"Mr. Henderson," she said, her mouth feeling like it was stuffed with cotton balls. "What's going on?" She'd been placed on her side on the facing seat, but when she tried to sit up she realized her hands were bound in front of her. Her ankles were also tied together.

"Would you care for a drink? You must be thirsty." Mr. Henderson pointed to a frosty bottle of water. It rested in a cup holder, sweating even in the cool confines of this lush vehicle.

She wasn't drinking anything he provided. "No thanks."

He laughed, sounding genuinely amused. "It's not drugged."

Clearing her throat, she shook her head. Time to be a handful. "Whatever. I'm not drinking it!" she said stridently, borrowing Justine's hard-core bitch tone.

"Suit yourself." He seemed unmoved by her attitude. His demeanor was as serene as if everything in his plan had worked out perfectly.

"Where are we going?"

"You'll see soon enough." He looked out the window. She also glanced around, trying to see if she recognized any of the terrain they were passing. It didn't look immediately familiar. They seemed to be driving out of town. She turned her head, looking toward where they were going instead of where they'd been.

In the distance she saw something quite alarming. A small airport.

They drove closer and closer. If he got her on a plane, she'd be gone forever.

CHAPTER 20

Deke called Zak to try and direct him to the airport, but he must still be on his way to the hospital from Chloe's workplace and didn't answer. He thought about contacting Jessica and setting the FBI loose on the situation, but she was only doing him a favor. She didn't have any actionable evidence to send anyone official his way to help. Perhaps The Organization, where Zak worked, had resources he could tap. He redialed Zak, getting his phone mail yet again. Was Zak stuck in traffic or something?

He raced down five flights of stairs and exited the hospital at the parking lot where the message had directed Chloe to go, although he suspected she'd been carried out on a gurney. Perhaps right past his nose as he spoke on the phone. He'd fallen one step behind the man he was certain was directing all of this. Mr. Edgar Henderson.

He hopped into his sports car, glad that he drove this vehicle today, and headed toward Baxter's Airfield at top speed.

Baxter's wasn't a huge place, but he didn't know what he was looking for either. Deke was miles from the airfield when he saw a small jet take off to the west and felt his belly lurch.

Was it Chloe and her abductor flying off to a country with no extradition? Was she already gone? Out of his reach? No.

He'd track her. He'd use every possible advantage to ensure he found her and rescued her. But a plan didn't materialize in his head in this frustrating moment. The sense of failure weighed on him like a shroud, smothering him. He hadn't protected the woman he loved beyond reason. He stomped on the gas, the view of the airport growing larger as another small jet took off heading in the opposite direction.

A couple miles from the airport, Deke succumbed to the various depressing details outlining his day. Chloe was missing. He couldn't get hold of Zak. Jessica had given him his foe on a silver platter, but Deke feared it was too late to do anything about it. Was it? Too late?

His foot mashed down on the brake. He was weighed down with useless despair and he needed to snap out of it. He wasn't too late. He would find her.

Deke pulled to the side of the empty road, willing himself to calm down and think through his options, select the best one and go forth to dominate. He dialed Zak's number. The call went to phone mail again. Where was his ever-on-the-spot brother? He was about to put the car back into drive and head for the airport when his phone buzzed in his hand.

Jessica. Maybe she had good news. He needed it. Deke transferred the call through the Bluetooth in his car, answering with, "What's up?"

"That flight I told you about took off early. Unless you've learned to teleport yourself using your mind, you couldn't possibly have made it to Baxter's from the hospital in enough time."

Deke stared out his windshield at the airport, nodding even though she couldn't see him. "You're right. I didn't make it. So please tell me you have good news."

"I have news. Can't guarantee it's good though."

"Tell me." Hope fluttered in his belly. Whatever this news was, he'd make it good.

"There were three companies connected in a hierarchy to the mystery drug you sent me. One was a shell company that's legit, as far as I can tell, but it turns out they also have a company jet registered and in regular use."

"Is it by chance taking a trip today?" he asked.

"Yes, indeed. The flight plan was filed weeks ago, but I had my feelers out to red flag anything having to do with a flight from any of the companies linked together. I just got a notification that the preflight information was started a few minutes ago. The flight is scheduled to leave in just under two hours."

"From where? Baxter?"

"No. This time it's Granger Airfield."

"And Granger Airfield is, of course, on the opposite end of town."

"Yep," she said. "At least this time you have time to make it there. Keep in mind they can always leave early, but I think this is a better chance."

"I hope so. But my success remains to be seen. I haven't been batting a thousand lately."

"No one bats a thousand, Deke."

He smiled, appreciating that his sister-in-law and favorite FBI agent was trying to cheer him up.

Deke put his car in gear and headed in the opposite direction. The good news was he knew a shortcut. The only bad news was he didn't know for certain that Chloe wasn't on the first flight, with this second one at Granger Airfield being used to send him on a chase down a rabbit hole.

"Thanks, Jessica. I'm on my way across town. And I owe you big."

"Awesome. That means bodyguard for baby services

coming my way," she said, amusement lacing her tone.

"Hey, can you check one other thing?"

"Sure. What's up?"

"Could you track down Zak? He was on his way to the hospital, but hasn't checked in yet."

"Let me ping his phone. Hang on."

After a few minutes she came back, sounding worried. "Uh, Deke."

"What?"

"Zak's phone is already headed toward Granger Airport."

Chloe was largely ignored as they got closer to the airport. She tried to use the time to her advantage by being hyper alert and watchful, and learned some interesting things. For example, both Mr. Henderson and his chauffeur, Klaus, were using cell phones.

Before today, she'd seen Mr. Henderson with a cell phone exactly one time. During their house hunt last year he'd needed to check something and pulled out the device like it was some form of alien technology he was reluctant to touch at all, let alone use with any sort of proficiency.

Today he tapped and swiped like a teenaged pro, working the smart phone like he was testing a new model before its release to the general public.

That was a very unusual sight indeed. Mr. Henderson wasn't the Luddite he'd always pretended to be. The fact that he'd apparently been trying to kidnap her for weeks was another big surprise. She'd believed he was simply a slightly eccentric, very wealthy widower trying to find a new city to settle down in with multiple properties to place in his name.

Mr. Henderson and Klaus sat at the back of the limo,

smiling and joking like old friends as they each wielded their cell phones with practiced efficiency. She had to hand it to them, the times she'd been in their presence before she'd been completely fooled by their act. What else had she gotten wrong about Mr. Henderson besides the obvious? Likely every single thing she'd counted as the truth.

A glance out the window showed Chloe they'd arrived at the airport. They drove to the far southern end of it to a remote area where four large hangers were lined up near a runway leading to the main airfield.

The unseen driver pulled into the open hanger door of the third one next to a small jet completely concealed by the large hangar. The nose of the jet was pointed toward the open doors as though it were ready to fly off at any moment. A heartsick feeling vibrated through her as she realized it was likely their transportation for the next leg of this unexpected journey, the one she didn't want to be part of.

Once the vehicle stopped, Klaus stepped out, closing the door behind him, and disappeared from sight. Oh goody. Perhaps she was about to find out what was going on.

A maintenance man in blue coveralls circled the jet, checking it out here and there along the fuselage. Chloe wondered if Mr. Coveralls knew what was going on or if he could be an ally. She tucked away the possibility of testing that theory once she exited the limo.

Mr. Henderson's voice startled her from her escape plans. "I feel like there is an elephant in the room. I'd like to be candid with you, if I may, Chloe," he said civilly. He glanced out the window at the jet being readied to fly.

"Please. I welcome your candor, Mr. Henderson." She suspected they were not even looking at a view of the same continent, let alone the same elephant.

"I was quite disappointed in what you did a while back." His voice was low and strained, like he fought to speak through strong emotions. She fought the desire to roll her eyes. "But then I realized you'd given up hope on the possibility of us, and so I forgave you." His tone turned magnanimous.

Her first thought was *what the fuck is he talking about*? She'd given up on the possibility of them? Whatever. The words "this man is cray-cray" repeated a few times in her head. How had she never caught on to his mental instability? Had he snapped recently or something? Had he ever been sane?

He turned, putting his focus back on her expectantly.

Chloe remained silent. No need to fan the crazy flames into a column of blazing insanity. The less she said the better. But she felt the need to respond and at least figure out the direction of his irrational thoughts and plans.

"When did you realize I'd given up hope?" she asked in a soft voice.

He smiled, seemingly pleased with her question. "It was several weeks ago at the baseball game. I was there that night. I know you must not have seen me because I couldn't get the seats I wanted, but I went there to save you from your date.

"Ned?"

An unpleasant frown formed on lips. "Yes. Him. I knew he wasn't right for you at all. Justine happened to mention she was setting the two of you up on a blind date when I was in her office a few days before that night."

"Justine told you about the blind date?"

"Yes. The poor thing has such a crush on me, but I told her, 'Chloe is the only one for me. She and I do very well together,' repeatedly to no avail. Unfortunately, she had to be dealt with in the end."

"*You* put Justine into that coma?"

Mr. Henderson's eyes widened in shock. "She's still alive? That's unexpected. I thought I had that dosage perfect." He shook his head as if in wondering disbelief. "Oh, well. No matter. She'll never figure out where we're going. She won't bother us anymore. We'll be safe. I promise you, Chloe."

"Where *are* we going?" she asked, then quickly added, "Where will we be safe?"

"Now, don't worry your pretty little head about the details, dear Chloe. I'll protect you." He frowned. "I'll certainly do a better job than that bodyguard you chose." He turned away as if in disgust of her recent security selection.

Deke's face filled her mind. She closed her eyes, unable to bear looking at Mr. Henderson when the person she most wanted to see was Deke. "He'll come after us," she said, suddenly worried about that very thing. "He's very serious about his job as a bodyguard." *Where are you, Deke? Do you even know I'm in trouble?* She tried to send a mental warning.

Mr. Henderson nodded. "I suspected as much. But I know his kind. He's only interested in the paycheck. He'll view it as his job to protect you. At least until you call him off." *What the…?* "Therefore, we'll have to ensure he knows you no longer require his services." *Oh, hell no!* Mr. Henderson seemed completely blind to the idea that she and Deke were a couple. Or was he?

"How will we do that?" Chloe's tone was perhaps a tad more belligerent than it should have been, given the level of cuckoo she was dealing with, but her anger was hard to subdue. "How can we get him to stop chasing after us, I mean?" she asked in a modified tone.

Mr. Henderson shrugged as if it was the easiest thing in the world. Perhaps in his world of insanity, merely wanting things a certain way guaranteed success. "Call him and fire him. Tell him you've found a new protector."

"He won't believe it. He has feelings for me."

Mr. Henderson nodded. "Yes. Given what's gone on, I suspected as much." His eyebrows went up as if he had a sticky problem to solve. "You've been a vixen and led him on, Chloe. Now there's no choice but to break his heart and leave him behind."

"What?"

"We will make a phone call and you will end it. Tell him you don't love him. Tell him he doesn't need to protect you anymore."

"I don't think he'll believe me." Chloe tried to imagine a few scenarios where she called Deke and told him she wanted to break things off, each one coming to a ridiculous conclusion. Either Deke would be emboldened to try harder to discover her location, or she'd scream and beg for him to come and get her at the airport as soon as possible. Either way Mr. Henderson would certainly discover her true loyalties.

Mr. Henderson leaned forward in his seat. His expression darkened to a sinister sneer. His tone was low when he said, "Then you must make him believe it, Chloe. Someone's life depends on it. You don't want to be responsible for someone being dead, do you?"

A chill literally ran down her body at the words *someone's life depends on it*. Chloe refused to ask the obvious, not wanting to find out it was her life that depended on convincing Deke to let her go.

What if Mr. Henderson's was a *come with me or die* proposition? Or an *if I can't have you no one can* sort of a plan? Would she have the courage to do whatever it would take to survive?

Disheartened by her grim prospects, she was distracted when the trunk of the limo opened and Klaus started removing luggage. One step closer to the private jet ride. Plus, she had to lie convincingly to the man she loved with all her soul.

Mr. Henderson pulled out a phone from his pocket. "Let's use this phone to call your bodyguard, shall we?"

Chloe shrugged, not looking at the device too closely. Mr. Henderson skillfully opened and promptly used the phone to dial a number using speakerphone. She heard one ring then two, and hoped he didn't answer. But of course he did.

Beyond the window she saw Klaus place his surprising burden on the ground outside of her door. She swallowed hard, now knowing exactly the life at stake in order to be convincing.

It wasn't her. Someone else's life was on the line.

Deke answered with a single-worded question, making everything very clear. "Zak?"

Deke had spent the better part of the last hour with his blood pressure spiking into the red zone as he did his best to find Chloe—or Zak—at the Granger Airfield. The first twenty minutes he'd sped across town using every shortcut he knew to arrive at his destination as fast as possible.

Even so, Granger was twice the size of Baxter and there were more than a few groupings of outlying buildings to search on the vast property perimeter, especially given his unknown but certainly limited allotment of time.

He kept moving, ever hopeful that he'd get lucky and find what he sought before the next—and possibly the final—flight took off.

Zak was here somewhere, too. Or his phone was. That was a whole different level of concern. Using the information Jessica had eventually forwarded to his phone, Deke saw something interesting in the group of buildings and hangars he currently drove by. He parked his sports car at the back corner of an abandoned hangar to explore his latest hunch on foot, noting grimly that his big SUV couldn't find as many good hiding places as his sports car could.

When the call came through displaying Zak's name, he wasn't quite ready to hear Chloe's voice at the end of his brother's phone line. Stunned for only a few seconds, Deke stepped up his game in light of what he'd discovered right before the call came in.

"Zak?" he asked, instead of hello, as usual. There was a pause on the line. Deke filled the space, asking, "Where have you been, bro? I've been looking for you."

"Deke, it's me," Chloe said. Deke, still searching on foot, stepped into a nearby hangar out of view to discover what was going on and why Chloe had called on Zak's phone.

"What are you doing on Zak's phone, Chloe? Is Zak with you?"

Chloe cleared her throat before speaking. She already sounded different or maybe off was the right word. "Listen," she said quietly. "That doesn't matter. I need you to hear me right now, Deke."

"Okay, I'm listening."

"This isn't working for me anymore."

Deke squinted. "I beg your pardon. What isn't working for you anymore?" He used his very best *what the fuck* tone of voice, too, as that was how he was feeling. Perhaps it was his blood pressure talking.

There was a short silence on the line. "Us," she said even more quietly. "What isn't working for me anymore is the two of us."

"I don't understand."

There was another gap of silence on the line. Chloe cleared her throat again and said haltingly, "The thing is,

Deke, I just don't love you the way you want me to. In fact, I never really loved you. It was all an act."

"I see. That's very surprising news."

"I never meant to lead you on or hurt you."

"Oh?" He laughed. "That's funny. Don't worry, Chloe. I always knew exactly what you were all about. You loved my big house and the rich life I maintain. You loved that I was famous. Oh, wait. Let me guess. Am I supposed to be heartbroken right now because you're breaking up with me?" He laughed again, as if he were amused by her sudden change of heart and surprising declarations.

She sounded a little hurt when she said, "I don't know. You're certainly taking this news much better than I expected." Her wounded tone came through loud and clear. That was okay. Maybe it was for the best.

"Kind of uncool of you to break up with me over the phone, but you know what?" Deke asked, not waiting for her to respond. "I don't care. My sister was right about you all along, Chloe. She never liked you from day one. She predicted you'd last a couple of weeks and then dump me for someone else with more money."

Chloe sucked in a deep breath. This time her response sounded angry. "Did she?"

"Yep. Chalk one up for Shelley."

Her tone hardened even more. "So that you know, I never liked your sister either."

"Whatever. Now what? Are you moving out right away? Should I just throw all of your stuff out on my lawn for you to pick up later?"

"Don't bother. I don't need it. In fact, I'm leaving today."

"Figures. So this is it, right? We're done? I can move on?"

"Yes. I'd say that's very accurate."

"Good." He hung up without saying good-bye.

Chapter 21

Chloe's eyes slid shut the moment Deke hung up. She failed to stifle the tears that came along with what she hoped was a performance. On some level she knew it was not real. Deke loved her, didn't he? Her captor looked confident that everything continued to go according to plan.

"That wasn't so bad now, was it? Looks like he never cared for you anyway."

"Sounds like it." Chloe eyed the phone, wishing to hear Deke's voice again. Only this time she wanted him to tell her he loved her. That he'd be devastated if she left him. That he didn't have a secret sister named Shelley who hated her.

He'd said that name before, hadn't he? She tried to remember. Wasn't Shelley his ex-girlfriend's name? With her head still muzzy and weird from being unconscious before waking up in this limo, it was more difficult to separate fabrication from the truth. Not to mention that the drug she'd been given was still making her woozy, even just sitting up right.

"All right, it's time to leave." Mr. Henderson motioned for her to exit the limo.

"Am I supposed to hop?" She pointed her tied hands

at her feet. The drug still coursing through her system would be challenge enough for walking.

He looked perturbed for a moment then pulled a pocketknife out of his jacket and cut the zip ties off her feet and hands.

"Just keep in mind what's at stake."

"Got it."

Chloe climbed out of the vehicle slowly, stumbling a couple of steps past a still unconscious Zak. The light-headed feeling persisted. Climbing out of the car and standing up didn't help. Zak was laid out on the ground, slumped on one side where Klaus had put him clearly in her view while she'd still been in the limo, chatting with Deke.

Zak looked like he'd suddenly gotten tired and put himself down for a nap on the hard concrete hangar floor. At least he seemed to be breathing. Klaus stood over him with a gun during the entire conversation with Deke. Now Klaus had relaxed. His gun was pointed at the ground by his foot, likely waiting for further instructions. Hadn't she just saved Zak's life by lying through her teeth about her feelings for Deke?

Chloe stumbled and Mr. Henderson grabbed her arm, then tentatively slung one arm around her shoulders. It took everything she possessed not to wrench herself away from him, dodging his unwanted touch.

She looked down at Zak, ensuring that his chest moved as he breathed.

"Where is the pilot?" Mr. Henderson released her as he turned to address Klaus. Chloe took the opportunity to take a half step away from Mr. Henderson's reach.

Klaus frowned, searching around the inside of the airplane hangar with an unhappy gaze. He shrugged. "Want me to go look for him?"

"No. Never mind. Take care of this matter first." He gestured toward Zak. "Get our things loaded into the aircraft and *then* go find the pilot so we can get in the air," Mr. Henderson demanded. "We need to get going. We've certainly waited long enough."

"What are you going to do with Zak?" Chloe asked, glancing down as she was pushed along. Mr. Henderson's hand was planted firmly on her lower back, shoving her along with every other step he took.

They walked a ways before he answered her. "I'm going to leave him behind for his brother to find."

"Alive, though, right?"

Mr. Henderson shrugged. "Not necessarily. That's the price owed for all the trouble your boyfriend bodyguard has cost me. We should have been gone weeks ago."

The sudden sound of a gunshot echoed in the hangar. Chloe shrieked, her knees buckling in startled surprise. She was terrified to look behind her and find that Klaus had just shot Zak. Oh no. An emotional wellspring of sadness erupted inside and she started to cry.

Mr. Henderson didn't even blink or look behind them.

"How could you do that?" she asked, sobbing in earnest. He grabbed her arm in his firm grasp and wrenched it upward in an effort to force her back to her feet. She cried out and struggled to get free, on her knees facing away from where Zak lay on the ground.

Mr. Henderson dragged her up. "Stop this right now. It's long past time to get on the plane and go, Chloe. Relax. Like I told you before. I'm taking you to a better life."

Chloe, sobbing loudly and still afraid to turn around, only took two small steps and continued to struggle. Her captor angrily yanked on her arm to get her to keep moving.

"Let's go." Over his shoulder, Mr. Henderson shouted, "Klaus! Find the pilot." He grabbed her arm again. She resisted. "Do you want me to put the restraints in place again? Come on. Cooperate."

Chloe took a single step forward and stopped. So many emotions were trying to escape she didn't know which to let loose. Anger. Betrayal. Sadness. Injustice. Her head drooped down.

"Klaus! Where are you?" Mr. Henderson started to turn, but someone came up behind them quickly.

"Stop." Deke's voice took her by surprise. She looked up and saw Deke held a gun pressed to the back of Mr. Henderson's head.

"Let go of her," he said with quiet authority. "You have quite a bit to answer for. Hurting my brother for starters."

Mr. Henderson released Chloe's arm and she stumbled backward a full step. His tone aggrieved, Mr. Henderson said, "He shouldn't have tried to stop us when we loaded Chloe into the limo at the hospital."

The sound of approaching cars filled the air, tires screeching to a halt just outside the hangar. She hadn't heard sirens, but now there were several police cars parked in front of the small jet they'd been about to board. Out of the lead car came Detective Pullman.

Deke kept his gun pointed at Mr. Henderson's face.

An approaching patrol officer called out, "Drop your weapon."

Deke took his focus off of Mr. Henderson, looking over one shoulder. "He ordered his man to kill my brother."

"No, I didn't." Mr. Henderson smiled as if he was about to turn this whole situation to his advantage. "My girlfriend and I were just leaving the country." He tried to wrap his arm around Chloe, but she dodged him.

"Don't touch me."

"Drop your weapon, Mr. Langston," Pullman said. "We have video of what took place in the warehouse."

"What video?" Mr. Henderson asked and spun to face the bevy of police officers moving closer to them. "They don't put video cameras in airplane hangars." He huffed a laugh, as if that were the most ridiculous thing he'd ever heard.

"Sure they do. With the price of surveillance so cheap these days, all insurance companies require it," Pullman said. "Please put the gun down," he repeated, but Deke was already bending to lower his weapon. He flipped the safety back on and placed the gun on the ground at his feet. At another firm order, he kicked it gently away with his foot.

A patrol officer picked it up. Deke looked at him and said, "I'm going to want that back."

Pullman rolled his eyes. "You'll get it back. Eventually."

Chloe relaxed as Mr. Henderson was handcuffed. He looked puzzled, as if he couldn't figure out why anyone was arresting him.

"My lawyer will have me out on bail like this." He snapped the fingers of both bound hands. "What are you charging me with anyway?" he asked Pullman.

"Attempted kidnapping, assault—"

"I didn't kidnap Chloe or assault her. She and I do very well together. I was taking her to a better place."

Chloe was about to argue, but Pullman said, "We haven't even cataloged the charges for this stunt yet. That's coming next. Currently, I'm talking about Justine Keller-Howe. She woke up from her coma twenty minutes ago. She told us everything you did to her. And while stranger things have certainly happened, I wouldn't count on any bail if I were you."

Mr. Henderson frowned again, as if he was still puzzled to be in handcuffs.

Chloe was relieved Justine had woken up.

She took one small, shuffling step closer to Deke. "I

want you to know that I lied before. I totally love you," she said, reaching for him.

Mr. Henderson watched angrily, becoming very agitated.

Deke dodged her touch and gave her a dirty look. The idea that he didn't want to hug her shocked tears into her eyes. Stupid drug making her weepy. But wasn't the time for playacting over? She retracted her unwanted touch with disbelief drilling all the way to her soul.

He turned to look at Zak, being tended by paramedics. He didn't look at her when he said, "I know how you feel, Chloe. Unfortunately, I wasn't lying before. We're done. I want you out of my house. You can pick up your things when I'm not home to see you."

He promptly moved away, never once looking at her as he headed toward his brother, still out cold on the floor. Deke squatted down, talking in low tones to the two paramedics.

"Serves you right," Mr. Henderson said as the officers started to lead him—or drag him one step at a time—to the waiting police car. "You should never have kissed him at that baseball game. You brought this all down on yourself, Chloe."

Chloe—still in shocked grief after Deke's abandonment—turned to Mr. Henderson with anger coursing through her veins. Her hands fisted at her sides and the fog of dizziness dissipated for the moment as fury rose within.

"How did I manage that, huh?" Somehow, Pullman was at her side. He put his hand on her arm, possibly to keep her from socking the old man in the jaw. She looked down to see her fists raised, ready to strike.

Mr. Henderson leaned forward, testing the boundary of his restraints, seemingly not caring if she punched him. "I was waiting for you that night at the baseball game. I was supposed to be the one to save you from that horrible blind date Justine set up. Me! Not him." He gestured wildly in Deke's direction. "Me! I was going to take you to paradise weeks ago, but over and over again you simply wouldn't cooperate with my repeated attempts to take you away to a better life."

Chloe opened her mouth to scream at him, but Pullman squeezed her forearm. "Don't antagonize him," he said. "Let him go. You can't use logic with crazy."

Mr. Henderson was shoved unceremoniously into the back of a police car as a patrolman read him his rights.

"I don't need my rights read to me. I have immunity because I'm rich and also I have lots of money," Mr. Henderson said to no one in particular, staring at Chloe with a gratified glint in his eye until the door closed. He was likely satisfied now that her life was completely ruined.

Pullman released her as Mr. Henderson was finally driven away and out of her sight. Chloe put her hands to her face, bent in half and cried, so grateful that he was gone. So happy to have been rescued. So miserable that she was alone.

She couldn't blame Deke for being mad about his brother. Was he really mad at her? He had saved her, but the muzzy feeling in her head made her unconvinced she'd ever win him back. Her outburst at Mr. Henderson had used up lots of energy. She wasn't even sure what was real and what wasn't.

Seconds later, she felt an arm around her shoulders. "I'm sorry, Chloe. I lied," Deke said. "I totally love you, too."

Chloe straightened and he pulled her into the tightest of bear hugs. "I really am sorry about that." Overcome with emotion and suddenly joyous that maybe they weren't over, Chloe sobbed into his collar.

She tightened her arms around his neck, not really caring why he'd done it. Like the remark about having a sister when she knew he didn't, she'd played along. But the drugs in her system seemed to pervert all her reason and logic into foolish emotional outbursts.

"Please don't cry."

She pulled away. "I don't want to. But I can't seem to help it. My emotions are on a rollercoaster. The drug he knocked me out with is making me lightheaded and also a big crybaby."

"I see. I'll just hug it out of you then." He held her tighter.

"I assume that whole fake breakup was for Mr. Henderson's benefit?"

"Yep. I figured he'd fight less going into custody if he felt like he'd succeeded in breaking us up."

"Probably. But drug-fueled, emotional outburst or not, I don't want to hear you say it ever, ever again, okay?"

He smiled and kissed her. "Okay."

"Now tell me the truth, the whole truth and nothing but the truth."

"I love you. Do we need a blood oath or something?"

"No. Just say it more. Say it a lot."

"I love you. I love you. I love you. And the truth is, no one could persuade me not to."

"Is this really over?"

"Yes. Well, we have to take Zak to the hospital. Turns out he was right. It *was* his turn to be unconscious, after all. Then I think we can go on with our lives."

"One last thing. Do you promise not to throw all my stuff on your lawn?"

Deke smiled, cupped her face in his hands and said, "I do."

From behind them, Zak said groggily, "Those are the two words that will not only get a bad boy like you into big trouble, they'll be the best you ever utter in your life. Take it from me."

Zak climbed off the gurney the two paramedics had just put him on, shook his head as if to break an early morning fog and staggered over, leaning heavily into Deke. Turning to Chloe, he said, "You okay, gorgeous?" He put a hand on her shoulder and Chloe tried to help hold him up.

The paramedics attempted to get him back on the gurney, but he just kept waving them off.

Chloe released Deke, wrapped her arms around Zak's neck and hugged him tight. "I'm so sorry you got stuffed into the trunk. I didn't even know you were in there."

"Course you didn't. You were already out cold by the time I got there."

They swayed on their feet and Deke had to steady both of them. "I'm still sorry."

"That's okay." Zak patted her on the back, swinging into her again, but caught himself. They held on to each other for support as the paramedics continued to press him back onto the gurney. "I'm sorry I didn't see the third guy in the ill-fitted suit when I charged into the situation on that abandoned loading dock back at the hospital."

"Did they shoot you with a tranquillizer, too?" Chloe asked.

"No. Zapped me in the back with a Taser when I got close enough."

"What situation?" Deke asked.

"Captain Crazy and his wonder twin were stuffing Chloe into the back of the limo." Zak glanced around the area. "Where did the driver guy in the bad suit get to anyway?"

Deke said, "I knocked him out and shoved him into a room back there." He pointed to a corner in the back of the hangar.

Chloe said to Deke. "How did you find us? I didn't even know where I was."

Deke said, "I got Jessica to track Zak's phone to this location."

"She's the one in the FBI, right?"

"Yep."

"Which brother is she married to?"

"Reece," he and Zak said at the same time.

"I haven't met him yet, have I?"

"Not that I know of," Deke said.

"And you haven't met Dalton either," Zak said. "That's Deke's twin."

Chloe's mouth fell open. "You have a twin brother?"

"Yes."

"Identical?"

"Nope. And I'm older by ten minutes, too."

Zak laughed. "Well, we all look like brothers, and no one who doesn't already know can ever guess correctly which two of us are the twins."

Chloe hugged Deke tighter. "I'm just glad I get to keep Deke."

"Me, too," Deke said, kissing her cheek.

"I want to be best man at the wedding. Unless you elope."

Deke said, "Garrett already called it at the baseball game."

Zak frowned and pretended to cry and rub his eyes in despair.

"Guess we have to elope then," Chloe said. "I don't want to cause a rift in the family."

"You're right. How about tonight?"

"Can I go, too?" Zak asked.

"You have to go to the hospital. Get on the gurney."

"I'm fine."

"No. It's your turn. Don't be difficult."

"You can't make me go." Zak crossed his arms, looking stubborn, but swayed on his feet.

"Oh, can't I?" Deke pulled out his phone and thumb-dialed a number. "Kaitlin? It's Deke. Your husband is being obstinate. He needs to go to the hospital to be checked out. Talk to him."

Zak said, "Dirty pool calling my wife, Deke."

Deke handed his phone over. "Whatever. I'm right."

Zak said into the phone, "Hey, baby. No, I'm fine. He's exaggerating." He listened for a few seconds, pushed out a sigh and climbed onto the gurney. "Yes. I'm on it. Yes. I'm going. Okay. I'll see you there." He crossed his arms and looked put-upon all the way to the ambulance.

"We'll follow you there," Deke called out as his brother was loaded in.

"Whatever," Zak said dejectedly.

Deke hugged Chloe to him. Then he picked her up in his arms and carried her to his sports car hidden behind the hangar.

"Where are you taking me?"

"To the hospital. Maybe you and Zak can get the same room and we can get a family rate."

"Wait. Really?" She wrapped her arms around his neck as he carried her.

"You were drugged again. Just be glad I'm not making you ride in an ambulance." He lowered her into the passenger seat.

"That's just because you don't want to let me out of your sight."

Deke laughed. "You're right. I won't ever make that mistake again."

Dr. Candy Crush made her an outpatient in the ER, gave her two large IVs of fluid to clear her system of the drug, and sent her home under Deke's watchful eye.

Zak got the same treatment, although the doctor tried to talk him into an overnight stay. Zak declined, swearing he'd go home and let his wife nurse him back to health. Kaitlin met them at the hospital, so it was like a double date in the curtained off ER room.

Later, when Deke finally got Chloe back to his home and tucked into bed, he asked, "You didn't really believe it when I lied and said I didn't love you, did you? I was trying to be so clever mentioning a fictional sister."

She shrugged. "On some level way down deep where my logic went to hide, I knew. But the fanciful, irrational, frightened part of me that the stupid drug tapped into was harder to convince."

"I'm sorry about that. I'm really sorry I didn't insist on going into that hospital room with you. Next time, the rules be damned. I'll attach myself to you."

"When I heard that gunshot behind me, I was horrified and seriously afraid you'd never forgive me for getting your brother killed."

"I grabbed Klaus and put him in a sleeper hold, but his gun went off in the process and hit a cardboard box full of brochures. I'm just grateful the bullet didn't hit you or Zak."

"Are we really getting married?"

"Yes. Name the place and time. Whatever you want."

She sighed. "I'd like to elope. It sounds exciting." She paused and slowly moved her gaze to his.

Deke took her hand, sandwiching it between his palms. "But."

"But my mom might be unhappy." She shrugged. "She may have a few dreams and schemes about her only daughter's wedding and what it might look like."

"Okay. So what do you want to do?" His grin meant she was free to do whatever.

She allowed a mischievous smile to shape her lips. "Did I hear you mention going to Key West soon?"

He nodded. "Two months."

"Maybe we could swing through the central part of Florida, pick up my parents along the way and get married in that tropical location you've been talking about."

Deke took her into his arms. "Great idea." Then he kissed her like he meant it, whispering, "I love you, love you, love you."

Chloe snuggled into Deke's arms, feeling like she'd come home to stay.

EPILOGUE

Key West – Two months later

Deke and Chloe strolled into his parents' vacation home in Key West, ready to share their good news. They'd made plans to get married in a small ceremony on the beach at sunset in one more day.

Apparently it was called a destination wedding. Chloe's mother had been ecstatic that they, first, hadn't eloped, and second, let her help with the tropical wedding plans. Deke had even invited Garrett. He and his wife were arriving later tonight. Deke had kept the nuptials a secret from his family, wanting to surprise them as two of his brothers had already done.

He thought he'd have to make promises or threats to get Zak to keep quiet, but Chloe had simply asked him politely to keep it a secret and he'd agreed. No threats required.

They'd flown to Orlando, rented a car and visited Chloe's parents on the way down to Key West. Her parents, especially her mother, were very happy and excited about the coming ceremony and were also due later tonight, as they'd opted to drive down in their own vehicle.

Deke and Chloe made their way through the house listening to what sounded like a baseball game in progress. Deke knew Zak and Kaitlin were already here, but not who else was in attendance.

In the living room, his entire family was huddled around the big-screen television watching something.

A familiar piece of music came up and the video's camera angle went to the audience, scanning wildly through throngs of people before stopping suddenly.

Zak said, "This is it. Watch."

The kiss cam footage came up on the seventy-five-inch screen of him and Chloe kissing for the first time in the stadium.

Everyone in the room reacted loudly to the kiss.

To get their attention, Deke said loudly, "So then I asked her to marry me."

All heads turned in his direction.

Zak asked, "What did she say?"

"Funny, Zak. She said yes and the wedding is tomorrow."

His mother squealed in delight. "You're actually having a wedding?"

Deke nodded. "Yep."

"You didn't already elope?"

He shook his head. "It's going to be a destination wedding on the beach at sunset. You're all invited. Dress casual."

His mother clapped her hands in delight. "Finally a wedding I get to attend." She stood up, walked past Deke and hugged Chloe. "Welcome to the family, Chloe."

A very pregnant Jessica stood and waddled over to congratulate them. "Hi. I'm Jessica."

Chloe hugged her. "Did you know that you're Deke and Zak's favorite FBI agent?"

"That's funny. I'm probably the only FBI agent they know." She laughed and then stopped, grabbed a surprised Chloe's hand and put her palm flat on the top of her belly. "Feel that? I think it's an elbow, or maybe a knee. Hard to tell, but cool, right?"

Chloe nodded. She looked up at Deke with an awe-filled expression that said she couldn't wait to be in the exact same condition.

Deke decided they should give *that* a valiant effort, starting on their honeymoon, tomorrow night directly after their sunset beach wedding.

THE END

BAD BOYS IN BIG TROUBLE

Nothing's sexier than a good man gone bad boy.

AVAILABLE NOW

Biker

Bouncer

Bodyguard

COMING SOON

Bomb Tech

BIKER

BAD BOYS IN BIG TROUBLE 1

Despite the danger, there are some definite pluses to undercover agent Zak Langston's current alias as a mechanic slash low-life criminal. He doesn't have to shave regularly or keep his hair military short. He gets to ride a damn fine Harley. And then there's the sweet, sexy lady next door who likes to sneak peeks at his butt. Yeah, that was a major plus.

Kaitlin Price has had the worst luck with men. As if her unearned reputation as a frigid tease isn't enough, she also has to deal with her stepsister's casual cruelty and taunting tales of sexual conquests she can only dream of. So Kaitlin has never been with a man. So what? So what…

So maybe the sexy bad boy next door would be willing to help her with that.

Gunfire, gangsters and a kidnapping weren't part of her Deflower Kaitlin plan. Good thing for her bad boy Zak is very, very good. At everything.

AVAILABLE NOW

BOUNCER

BAD BOYS IN BIG TROUBLE 2

DEA Agent Reece Langston has spent a year at the city's hottest club, working his way closer to the core of a money laundering operation. Women throw themselves at him all the time, but there's only one he's interested in catching. And she won't even tell him her name.

FBI Agent Jessica Hayes doesn't know much about the sexy stranger except that he's tall, dark and gorgeous. Best of all, he seems just as drawn to her as she is to him—in other words, he's the perfect man to show one kick-ass virgin what sex is all about. No names, no strings and no regrets.

Their one-night stand turns into two. Then a date. Then…maybe more.

Everything is going deliciously well until Jessica's boss orders her to use her lover to further an FBI operation.

Everything is going deliciously well until Reece's handler orders him to use his lover to get closer to his target.

Is their desire enough to match the danger and deception?

ABOUT THE AUTHOR

Fiona Roarke lives a quiet life with the exception of the characters and stories roaming around in her head. She writes about sexy alpha heroes, using them to launch her series, *Bad Boys in Big Trouble*.

Find Fiona Online:

www.FionaRoarke.com

www.facebook.com/FionaRoarke

Printed in Great Britain
by Amazon